The Secret Adv

Book 4

Jewel Dog and the Dragons

By Debi Evans

Illustrations by Chantal Bourgonje

Edited by Emma Corbett

For Rhiannon

www.debievans.com

Debi Evans

Rolo

Published by Debi Evans
First Edition published in 2017
Printed by Biddles
Blackborough End, Norfolk

ISBN 978-0-9928257-6-8

For my dear dad, Grandad Polo, and for Helen and Sheelin who unwittingly became part of Rolo's secret adventures.

In case you haven't met him, Rolo is a rescue Jack Russell and also the 'chosen one', discovering he has the ability to time travel via a hidden passage in an oak tree whenever he brings his pink ball. He is sent on secret adventures by Athelstan, tree dragon and guardian of the forest and aided by Yulia and Da, tiny woodland folk and Bubo the owl.

Rolo travels back through history to witness and sometimes influence events - Unbeknown to his owners: the smiley lady and the floppy haired boy, who wonder why their lovable pet is often tired during the day!

Life with Rolo is a constant adventure and his antics provide plenty of material for his blogs. Inspiration for chapter content can be sparked by hearing a news item, watching a documentary, listening to a podcast, laughing at social media 'funnies' and especially listening to requests from Rolo's readers – hence Greek mythology and more mythical creatures in this latest adventure. Also by actual events.

Contents

Prologue... 7

Chapter 1 Rolo and the Red Kites...................... 8

Chapter 2 Rolo revisits the Bronze Age............ 24

Chapter 3 The Christmas Truce of 1914........... 48

Chapter 4 Rolo and King Alfred the Great....... 73

Chapter 5 The founding of the UAE 1971........104

Chapter 6 Rolo and Montgomery Castle......... 126

Chapter 7 Rolo and the Jewel Collar.................135

Chapter 8 Rolo and the Trojan Horse...............142

Chapter 9 Rolo and the Cardiff Dragon...........165

Chapter 10 Rolo in the Underworld..................188

Chapter 11 Rolo and Aesop's Fables................. 213

Chapter 12 Gwyn lost...225

Chapter 13 Rolo and the Unicorns...................237

Chapter 14 Rolo to the Rescue...........................263

Postscript...281

www.debievans.com

Prologue

One minute I'm bounding through the long grass, the spiky new growth tickling my tummy, then my strides are getting longer – and l o n g e r – quite an achievement for short legs I can tell you! All of a sudden I can't feel the ground beneath my paws anymore – it's as if I am treading water in the air! Wowee! I'm flying! My front paws are moving of their own accord now, not diagonally opposite with back paws like Spotty Dog (ask mum or dad who that is if you don't know; he's a legend), but rhythmically beating time up and down as if they were wings.

Hold the front page – they ARE wings! This is surely a dream! I'm a rescue Jack Russell who time-travels and blogs. I've only ever been a passenger before now, flying across the sky with Rhydian the Welsh dragon, and here I am soaring through the air under my own steam!

From the corner of my eye I just catch the jewel collar around my neck glowing.

The Secret Adventures of Rolo

Chapter 1

Rolo and the Red Kites

I was out for a walk with the floppy haired boy and we bumped into Chickpea, a neighbouring Jack Russell and great pal of mine. We greeted each other warmly and were soon running around playing our dog version of tag called 'I wee, you wee'. We were up the hill on top of the college playing fields and the floppy haired boy started chatting to the girl who was walking Chickpea.

We terriers had raced on ahead and were about to enter a small copse, excited to be outdoors following a fresh scent and delighting in each other's company, when suddenly I heard a tremendous flapping of wings and a mournful, keening cry. A dark shadow loomed overhead and then a huge bird swooped down and made straight for us.

Chickpea couldn't believe her eyes and was barking frantically, jumping up at the winged assailant in a valiant attempt to stave off the attack. We were too far ahead for our humans to hear the commotion and come to our aid.

The bird's great talons didn't even touch the ground. I glance back over my shoulder as I ran and realised he was targeting me and zooming in, feet first! The mighty claws deftly closed around the straps of my red harness without touching my body.

The Secret Adventures of Rolo

The big bird of prey put his inbuilt engine into reverse and I found myself suddenly airborne as he ascended vertically and silently, with me dangling beneath as we flew over the school rugby posts, skimming the tops of the tall beech trees and away from the playing fields. All of this seemed to happen within the blink of an eye.

Glancing down I could see a moving dot getting smaller and smaller; a barking Chickpea running round in circles and an oblivious floppy haired boy and girl still some distance from the frantic dog and the scene of my abduction.

I was certainly not willing to become bird food and stole a glance upward at my raptor captor and took a deep calming breath like I've seen the smiley lady do on the yoga mat. This couldn't be the end of my adventure – it had only just begun!

I realised by the bird's reddish-brown body and forked tail that my kidnapper was a red kite. Its powerful brown and white wings appeared to have

10

finger-like fronds at the ends of them and these powered the bird forward with every beat. The head, by contrast, was greyish white in colour and the beady eye that I could see was focused on flying dead ahead – but where was the kite taking me? I found myself thinking that it was just as well the smiley lady had tightened the straps of my harness when she fitted it that morning, or I might have slipped out and plummeted to earth from a great height!

To my amazement the bird turned its head to survey my dangling body, winked its beady eye at me and then spoke,

'I take it you ARE Roro are you not? I haven't picked up the wrong dog I hope?' I was taken aback by the bird's question. Roro? It was only Gwyn who addressed me by that name! But before I had a chance to answer, he continued,

'I have a trespasser in my nest amongst my brood. Small, white, scaly and not at all bird-like save for

11

having wings. I asked him his business and he kept saying 'Roro' over and over again. He seemed too exhausted to fly back to wherever it was he came from. I asked around via the kite communication system and eventually heard that the woodland folk had lost a baby dragon. They had been most anxious about him and were thrilled to learn I'd found him and asked if I could please return him as they couldn't come themselves to collect him just now.

'Roro is the name he calls you and I had a description, so I set off at once to find you. I would have brought him to you but he seems petrified of me. My offspring find him amusing. I've left him doing a spot of babysitting with my wife Milva. Sorry if I scared you by dognapping you just now. Do you think your humans will be worrying about you?' he asked.

Aha! The penny dropped and it all started to make sense. Gwyn was the white baby dragon I had brought back as an egg from the Iron Age as instructed by Rhydian, and hatched secretly in the airing cupboard. I had hidden him in the garage for a while and then taken him to Athelstan the tree dragon. Yulia and Da the woodland folk found him a cave for safe keeping whilst he grew stronger and learnt how to fly and how to fend for himself and, well, just be a dragon.

Yulia and Da and Bubo the owl had been having a bit of trouble with Gwyn in the wood as the dragon hatchling was growing quite rapidly, and the last I heard was that he was testing his wings, eager to fly off and explore on his own. It seemed probable that, longing for adventure, he may have flown away from the safe cave, travelled too far and now couldn't remember his way back to the forest.

I doubted the floppy haired boy had even noticed my absence – he had been too busy chatting to the girl walking Chickpea. He would perhaps assume I'd gone off chasing a rabbit and would find my own way home; I'd done that before.

The kite said he was called Jory and that it wasn't

far to his nest. He made a mewing "weoo – weoo
– weoo" sound as he approached a tall tree and
dropped me abruptly into a large bowl made of
twigs and lined with grass.

14

I fell into a soft cushion of what appeared to
be sheep wool and sure enough, there was the
mischievous dragon Gwyn puffing little sparks
and amusing the kite fledglings with his antics. I
untangled myself from the ungainly heap I had
landed in and tried not to step on anyone as I
wriggled to right myself.

'Roro!' the dragon greeted me with affection and I
couldn't help noticing an assortment of 'toys' in the
kite nursery, including crisp packets, rags and even
a handkerchief. There were three baby birds – well
they don't really look much like babies as they are
quite large and fluffy with alert round eyes, and now
all three were looking at me suspiciously. I hope they
didn't think I was a wiggly worm delivery straight to
their nursery for lunch!

Their father Jory was perched on the edge of the
nest and he nuzzled his offspring affectionately, each
in turn. I could see having a baby dragon in the
nest was causing a bit of an overcrowding problem
as there wasn't much room, especially with all the

decorations!

'My wife and I will fly you both back home. Milva will carry Roro and I will manage the winged young rascal.' Turning to his babies he added,

'Now you three, keep low down in the deep nest and be quiet or the bogey man will get you; we won't be long and we will bring back something tasty to eat.'

I thought the babies looked disappointed that 'Roro' wasn't their lunch.

'Bogey man?' I asked.

'That's what all parents threaten when they want their children to behave. We red kites are now a protected species and not as endangered by hunting or egg stealing as we once were. Farmers don't mind us – we don't kill pheasants or worry sheep. We mainly feed on road kill and the odd small mammal. Our feet are a bit too weak to wrestle with anything larger than a rabbit.' Jory whispered to me.

'Well, you managed to dognap this Jack Russell with yours!' I couldn't help replying. Jory was proud of the unusual strength in his legs.

Milva was slightly smaller than her husband and she pulled a thread from the side of the nest with her beak, unravelling what appeared to be a longish piece of string. Deftly she wove it around Gwyn's little scaly body, fashioning a sort of cocoon. When she was satisfied with her handiwork she stepped aside and Jory picked up the harnessed dragon, dangling the string cradle from his powerful beak.

'It's all right Gwyn, these birds aren't going to harm you,' I reassured the anxious dragonling who was whimpering in fear.

Milva inclined her head towards me as if seeking my permission and then picked up my harness in her beak. Both kites launched from the sturdy side of the large nest and once again I found myself airborne, with the squeaking of the young kites fading as we headed homeward, replaced by the excited squawks of 'Roro' from Gwyn dangling just in front of me. What a sight we must have been from the ground!

I soon spied the college playing fields below and directed Jory and Milva a little bit further west to the home of the smiley lady. I just had to hope that I could smuggle Gwyn into the garage again and keep him safe and undiscovered until night time when I could return him to the care of the woodland folk. We couldn't go straight to the cave as I wasn't sure if I'd been missed at home and was anxious to 'reappear' before the smiley lady sent out a search party for her beloved pet.

Oh no! The smiley lady was in the garden, sweeping up leaves and snipping dead flower heads. I could hear her having a conversation with the floppy haired boy through the open kitchen door.

'What do you mean, you've lost Rolo?' She put down the rake and stood with her hands on her hips, her back to the garden fence.

'Quick! Just set us down at the bottom of the decking and I will take over from here. Oh and thank you!' I called up to our winged transport. Luckily Gwyn was still encased in his makeshift cradle, so I pounced on the ends of it to make sure he didn't try to run off. We waited for a moment behind a large Chinese pot planted with bamboo. The baby dragon was struggling to break free and I was shushing him.

'Mum! Look behind you! There's a pair of kites swooping down over the garden! Do you think they're after next-door's rabbits?'

I held my breath. The smiley lady ran indoors – this was my chance. I half carried Gwyn around the side of the house to the garage. The door was locked. I panicked. The tool shed would have to do.

'Mum! Rolo's here! He's got something in his mouth!'

'I hope it's not wildlife,' said the smiley lady

anxiously from round the corner, waving binoculars. I stuffed Gwyn in the shed and flipped the latch just as the pair of them rounded the corner. I heard a thump as the dragonling must have knocked over a stack of flowerpots in the shed and saw a piece of thread disappear under the wooden door.

'Rolo, where have you been you naughty boy?' said the floppy haired boy as I jumped up to lick his face and crossed my paws that Gwyn would have the sense to keep quiet in his temporary accommodation. I burrowed my head in the boy's neck; he tickled my ears and I knew I was forgiven and the baby dragon was safe, for now. All I had to figure out was how to return him to the woodland folk who must be very worried indeed by now.

As luck would have it the floppy haired boy took me to the forest that afternoon and I managed to get a message to Yulia when he wasn't looking. She replied from between the tree roots that she would bring Bubo that evening to help her retrieve Gwyn from the garden shed.

Now, those of you who follow my adventures may recall that Father Christmas gave me a jewelled collar as a reward when I helped him sort out a problem with his reindeer. This jewel collar was taken by Rhydian the Welsh dragon as payment for a dragon ride – you can find this adventure in Book 3 'The Dragon's Pram'. What an exciting adventure it was, although I must admit it was very scary clinging on to the dragon's neck as we hurtled across the night sky. And I remember thinking at the time, much as I like flying, I'd rather be doing it under my own steam than as a passenger.

When I woke up in my basket in the kitchen the next morning, I felt something digging into my ribs, and further inspection showed it was the very same collar with the large clear crystal embedded in the centre of it. I wondered how it had got there and quickly hid it under my cushion, as I could hear the smiley lady rattling the door handle, about to let me out into the garden.

After an exciting day barking at squirrels, barking

The Secret Adventures of Rolo

at the postman, barking at the cats and visiting
Grandad Polo – no barking I hasten to add – at last
it was bed time and I had the opportunity to take
out the jewelled collar and inspect it more closely.
Had Rhydian visited? I wondered.

I carried the jewel collar carefully in my mouth
and placed it on the tiled floor. When I was sure
the house was quiet I opened the cupboard door
under the sink, moved the bottles of cleaning stuff
and the bucket and rubber gloves and twisted the
ring to open the secret trapdoor behind the u-bend.
I picked up the collar again with my teeth, went
through the hole and pulled the cupboard door shut
behind me.

Out in the night air, I ran quickly down the garden
steps, squeezed under the gate and trotted through
the forest along the familiar path and under the
bushes to the clearing where I knew I would find
Athelstan. I hoped the tree dragon might know why
the collar had reappeared in my basket.

I heard a creak and a groan and the dragon materialised in front of my eyes in his usual position, wrapped around the bark of the ancient oak tree that hides the entrance to the time tunnel.

'So little pup, the time will soon come for you to use the jewel collar,' the tree dragon smiled down at me, acknowledging what I had brought to show him.

'What do I need to do?' I asked eagerly.

'Nothing yet,' he replied. 'You will know when the time is right, that is why Rhydian has returned it to you. Keep it safe for now.' Athelstan was as annoyingly mysterious as ever!

With that, the dragon faded into the bark. No sign of him at all, just a very gnarly old tree. Frustrated I lifted my back leg against the knotty roots.
'ROLO!' I heard a roar like distant thunder from the spot where the tree dragon had disappeared. I straightened my back leg and trotted home with a little smile on my furry face.

Chapter 2

Rolo revisits the Bronze Age

I was dozing under the dining table with my left ear raised. I could hear the floppy haired boy shuffling about with his homework diary and sorting his pencil case and it occurred to me that he wasn't doing very much in the way of writing. I wondered if the smiley lady was easily fooled.

'Mu-m,' he addressed the smiley lady.
'Yes love,' she replied absentmindedly whilst concentrating hard on a crossword puzzle clue.
'Have you heard about the recent excavation of an important Bronze Age Settlement in East Anglia?'
The smiley lady put down the pen and took off her glasses.

'No, tell me about it,' she said encouragingly.
'Well, just before the turn of the century in 1999, long before I was born, an East Anglian archaeologist discovered a series of wooden posts sticking out of a quarry.

24

'Further investigation revealed the most important Bronze Age Settlement ever discovered in Britain and in 2005 Must Farm was partially excavated. The intention I think was to study and log the finds and then allow nature to continue to preserve the historic site in the Fenland mud, but it was soon realised that exposure to the air sped up the decay of these 3,000-year-old relics and so the decision was taken to fully excavate the site between 2015 and 2016.

'It's interesting because the discovery has changed the way we think about people in the Bronze Age and how they lived.'

'Wow, that's amazing!' the smiley lady enthused, 'but why did the artefacts start to disintegrate?'

'Because they had been preserved in the mud for centuries; can you believe things like woven cloth fibre, food in bowls, thatched roof and floor coverings remained intact. The real mystery though, and what my homework question's about, is what happened at Must Farm, because it seems to have been destroyed by fire, and the inhabitants fled rather rapidly and never returned to rebuild their homes.'

'How exciting!' said the smiley lady and they started to discuss possible reasons.

My ear went down and I really did go to sleep then, dreaming of Flint, the dog I had met in Amesbury during my last Bronze Age adventure.

Later that night, when the house was quiet and I'd been tucked up in my basket and told to be a good boy with no woof woofs in the night, I crept out, tiptoed across the kitchen floor and opened the cupboard under the sink. I manoeuvred the obstacles in my way and through the trapdoor I escaped to the great outdoors.

Down the garden steps I bounded two at a time – no time to greet next door's rabbits – under the gate and into the forest, along the path, under the bushes and at last to the foot of the great oak tree to find Athelstan the tree dragon.

Athelstan took a while to reveal himself to me and I thought at first he was playing a joke, but he said he had been in a deep sleep.

'Well what brings you here Little Pup?' he boomed affectionately. 'Can't you sleep?'

'The floppy haired boy has an interesting history question for his homework and I wondered if you might know the answer?'

'I'm all ears Little Pup,' the dragon smiled, stroking his jaw with his left claw which in my opinion only added to his air of wisdom.

I explained to the tree dragon about the Bronze Age Village at Must and he listened and nodded sagely. 'Then I think you MUST go there and see for yourself,' Athelstan guffawed at his little joke. 'Did you bring the orb?'

I retrieved the pink ball from its hidey hole at the base of the tree as this was the key to my entering the time tunnel. Without the pink ball, the entrance would not open. As if by magic, Yulia and Da the woodland folk appeared holding their tiny lanterns aloft, ready to light my way.

'Where are we off to Paddy Paws?' smiled Yulia as I bent down so she could stand on a tree root and scratch behind my ears the way I liked it best. Athelstan explained the location and exact moment in time needed and Yulia nodded, ushering me towards the time tunnel.

'Ooh, that's a long way away and a long way back in time,' grumbled elderly Da, rubbing his back as he plodded slowly towards the entrance.

'I can take Paddy Paws on my own, Da, you don't have to come,' volunteered Yulia stepping into the hole, but Da was having none of it.

'Keep your eyes open and beware of dragons!'

whispered Athelstan as he faded to become part of the tree bark once more.

I'm not sure what he meant by that remark – but I kept it in mind.

The journey through the narrow passages of the underground time tunnel seemed to take forever – Da was right – it was a long way to go to East Anglia and a long way back in history. We discussed happenings in the forest to pass the time: the coming of spring and the appearance of wild garlic poking its green shoots up through the leaf mould covering of the forest floor. I had learnt from the woodland folk that it was called the 'understory', as opposed to the 'canopy' which was the tree tops. When we emerged into the sunlight, the first thing I noticed was that the air seemed cooler and there was water all around us but I couldn't smell the sea. We appeared to be inland.

'We will wait in the time tunnel entrance, Paddy Paws. Off you go and do what you have to do,' said

Yulia as she waved me off.

Well the first thing I had to do was have a wee, but enough about that; I don't want to bore you with too much detail.

I could see several large round huts ahead of me and what struck me as unusual was that they were raised up on wooden stilts and built on top of the water. I think I counted seven dwellings in total. It puzzled me at first as to why villagers would build their huts over the water and then I saw a number of long wooden boats loaded up with goods plying backward and forward along the waterways. I wondered if this place was linked to the rest of Britain and perhaps even further afield to mainland Europe by water.

Yulia had told me on our journey that this Bronze Age settlement in East Anglia was very like those found in Germany, Holland and Switzerland dating from the same era (1000BC). It seemed likely that these foreign nations traded together long before

Europe was established. Indeed, exotic beads recently found at Must Farm confirmed the belief that the dwellers enjoyed wealth and trade with other countries. I had gleaned this bit of information from the floppy haired boy's homework hand-out which he had left lying on the table.

Unobserved, I climbed up into one of the roundhouses and immediately noticed a large wooden wheel on a spindle lying flat just off the floor. I'd never seen the likes of this before and couldn't wait to report back to Athelstan – I thought wheels had come into use much later in history. I wondered what its purpose was in this hut and thought it was perhaps used for grinding cereal crops, but I heard footsteps approaching so couldn't hang around to find out.

Outside the hut I had a good look at the materials that had been used to construct the different dwellings. This round building was a detached wooden structure with what looked like hazel branches interlocking around circular posts to make

31

walls, and water reeds woven together to make a kind of thatched roof. Thanks to my nature lessons from the woodland folk I was able to identify these plants. Inside there was a rush mat floor covering, like an ancient carpet. 'All highly flammable', the health-and-safety-aware side of me thought.

I could tell by items of clothing laying around that the dwellers appeared to be well dressed: certainly their clothes were finer than those worn by the Amesbury folk I had previously met. I'm no expert but I would guess they were made from woven plant fibres which gave them a depth of texture and an appearance of quality.

I peered into another hut and saw someone working hard with a flax stem beater, and two women were winding bobbins with newly spun thread. This was a great hive of industry – so much for the myth that Bronze Age Britain was backward. This settlement seemed to me to be very progressive indeed.

Outside a third hut I observed a group of men

honing their shiny bronze swords, still steaming from the blacksmith's fire where they had been forged by pouring molten metal into a mould. I remember the floppy haired boy marvelling that it took one kilo of bronze to make one sword. I watched the muscular blacksmith at work with admiration.

This was a very wealthy group of people and they were well-armed. A thought occurred to me: were they perhaps expecting an invasion? Those heavy swords were surely made for killing not hunting. Did these people feel threatened and were they sensing danger? From whom might they be expecting an attack? The waterways were no doubt useful for trade but might make them vulnerable to invasion by foreigners. Were these dwellers themselves traders or invaders? The water would have linked them to other settlements along waterways such as the Trent or the Thames or further abroad across the sea. Were other people jealous of their apparent wealth? There were so many questions racing around in my furry head.

I didn't have long to wait to find out what happened here. Athelstan was always very accurate with pinpointing the right time in history to send me to. I settled myself behind one of the huts and pondered what might have caused this place to become deserted in a hurry, and why it had collapsed into the mud of the river it straddled.

I must have dozed off, enjoying a little power nap, because the next thing I heard was the rhythmic beating of wings. It sounded very much like an approaching dragon and I was not disappointed! In fact there were two dragons, different looking, one red and one white, roaring and breathing fire and swooping at each other as if they were in some kind of aerial combat. This was terrifying! It was all very well Athelstan telling me to look out for dragons but how was I expected to stay safe? They didn't seem at all friendly.

Time and time again the dragons clashed and scorched each other's scaly armour-plated bodies and roared at each other as neither gave way in their relentless attack. I wondered what they were fighting over.

The Secret Adventures of Rolo

The terrified villagers came flocking out from the roundhouses, glanced up at the sky and fled the scene, grabbing weapons as they ran. They left everything else behind them in their hurry to escape the dragon fight. I had the impression this wasn't the first time they had seen warring dragons overhead. Pots were overturned, livestock abandoned and jewellery scattered in the frantic panic of escape. Men, women and children jumped into their flotilla of log boats and beat their oars as if their lives depended on it. This was a mass evacuation.

I watched open-mouthed from my vantage point behind a tree, marvelling at these two mighty creatures fighting in the sky. I was distracted from this awesome spectacle when I started to feel an intense heat very close by and realised in horror that in their battle the careless dragons had set fire to the thatched roofs of Must settlement!

The roundhouses caught fire easily from the fiery dragons' breath and were soon burning fiercely, and as they burned the structures were collapsing on

their stilts and falling into the water below.

It only took a matter of minutes – probably no more than ten in all – for the Bronze Age settlement to be reduced to a pile of smouldering timber, lying sizzling in the water. There were no humans left at the scene, only two very angry dragons and this small four-legged eye-witness.

Finally the fire breathers seemed to call some sort of truce by making a signal pointing their wings: first the white dragon and then the red dragon came swiftly down to land just in front of the tree I was hiding behind. These dragons had no knowledge of the extent of the chaos and devastation they had caused by their quarrel.

'Come on, Rolo, YOLO 'You Only Live Once' – that is what the floppy haired boy often said to me and I said it out loud to bolster my courage as I stepped out to confront them both.

'Look what you two have done! You've completely destroyed a whole village! What on earth are you fighting about?'

Both dragons span round and looked at me angrily and the white one spoke first,

'It's a long running battle between we two – we fight the length and breadth of Britain.'

'But why would you do that?' I asked.

'For territory!' They said in unison.

'He started it,' snarled the red dragon.

'No, you did,' countered the white.

The pair sounded like arguing children to me. I
wanted to add,

'...and I'm going to finish it,' like I'd heard the smiley
lady say to resolve an argument.

'I am the rightful dragon of Britain. The English
call me Reod, but I am Welsh by birth,' said the red
dragon.

'And I am Alba,' piped up the white dragon puffing
out his chest. 'I am the rightful dragon of Britain
being English by birth.'

Well, well, I thought to myself. So, there were more
dragons flying around than the old red one and the
young white dragonling that I knew!

'I think you two had better be more careful where

you carry out your skirmishes.'

I drew myself up to full height and bravely squared up to the dragons, 'Otherwise you're going to wipe out the whole of Britain and then neither of you will be the rightful dragon of anywhere!'

The dragons looked at me suspiciously. Then Reod said,

'Take care, docga, for although small you would make a tasty snack and we are hungry.'

The dragons took to the air; dive bombed towards me skimming over the top of my head and then shot off in a westerly direction.

'See you over the Marches,' shouted Reod the red. '…and I'd like to see you try and defend them next time!' shouted Alba the white, tilting his wings in a defiant gesture.

I thought I'd handled that rather well.

'Dragons 1 - Humans 0,' I muttered, trying to quell my terrier shake as I headed back to the time tunnel entrance, casting a final look over my shoulder at the huts that were sinking fast into the river. I was pleased to see the twinkling welcome of Yulia's lantern in the entrance to the time tunnel.

'Shouldn't we do something about putting the fire out?' I asked the woodland folk, voicing my concern about the burning village.

'Don't worry, the river is taking care of it,' said Da, and sure enough the village was soon engulfed by water, dousing the flames and leaving little trace, just the smell of burnt timber in the air and a wisp of smoke rising from the water. This village would lay undiscovered by man for the next 3,000 years.

∽∽∽

'Haven't you finished your homework yet?' I heard the smiley lady ask the floppy haired boy at the weekend.

'Well, judging by all the bronze swords that were

found at the place, I reckon the village was attacked and the inhabitants probably fled by boat,' the floppy haired boy replied and then added, 'but that doesn't explain the scorch marks on the remains of the timber found in the river mud, nor does it account for why the villagers never returned to rebuild nor why the invaders didn't settle in the place they had conquered.'

I could tell the floppy haired boy was not very happy with the wishy-washy conclusion of his homework. I wished I could share with him my first-hand knowledge. Wouldn't he love to know that Must Farm was accidentally destroyed by Reod and Alba fighting over the right to be recognised as the supreme dragon of Britain!

Rolodogblog #1

I've learnt a bit more about blogging by watching the floppy haired boy. He uses lots of hash tags, so I've started using them too in my blogs in this book.

Now, I'm going to share with you a great adventure story which I heard the smiley lady re-telling, about a black Labrador called Beauty. She lived in a farmhouse in Buckinghamshire and was in the garden one day when a deer ran straight across the flowerbeds and Beauty gave chase. The deer leapt over a low hedge, ran out on the road and the Labrador chased it a fair way but lost sight of the deer when it ran into a farmer's field.

43

The Labrador didn't recognise the place she had run to and was exhausted from the chase. She sat down on the pavement panting, waiting for her owners to find her. After a while a big red double decker bus called a 'route master' came along — one of those old-fashioned buses that is open at the back so you can jump on and off even when it's moving.

Beauty watched a few people get off the bus and then followed a lady with a shopping basket on wheels as she climbed on-board. The Labrador knew she wasn't allowed to sit on the bench seats so she settled for the big stairwell under the curving staircase which led to the upper deck — the space where people normally store their luggage. She just lay there on the floor panting, much to the concern of the passengers on the bus. The conductor came along with his ticket machine which made an alarming whirring sound every time a ticket shot out, but Beauty had no money and anyway she didn't know where she wanted to go.

The bus conductor was bemused by the situation, pushed back his peaked cap and scratched his head, deciding to let the dog have a free ride as she seemed to have settled down quite comfortably. The passengers tried to guess how she had got there.

When the bus reached the end of its route in the next town, the kindly bus conductor who had finished his shift for the day, took off his tie and used it to make a lead around Beauty's neck and took her to the local police station. The duty sergeant wasn't quite sure what to do with Beauty as she wasn't wearing a collar with a tag with her home details, and so he locked her in a cell to keep her safe whilst he made some enquiries. Beauty was anxious to go home but was now shut in. She would have to sit and wait until her owners came searching for her.

Several hours later, Beauty's distraught owner rang the neighbouring police station,

'I've lost my black Beauty,' the woman sobbed down the phone, 'have you found her?'

'Well, madam, we don't have a

horse here, but we do have a black Labrador. It got on a bus and wanted to go to Barking.'

The policeman laughed heartily at his own joke. The poor owner was too upset to see the funny side and hurried to reclaim her adventuring dog and take her home. No harm done but from that day onwards Beauty wore a collar with her owner's telephone number on it, just in case she went adventuring again. I had to ask Athelstan to explain the joke.

#bustobarking

Chapter 3

Rolo and the Christmas Truce of 1914

One day the floppy haired boy and I were out walking in the forest and I spied something under some bushes. I stared at it for a bit and then started barking with excitement.

'What is it, Rolo?' said the floppy haired boy, parting the branches and leaning in for a closer look.
The object was flat but not rigid. I could get my teeth round it to retrieve it.

'Fetch, Rolo. There's a good boy,' encouraged the floppy haired boy, holding out his hand, eager to see what I had found.

I dropped the strange object at his feet.

'Why, it's an old football. No air in it at all, not much use. We can't play with this. It's more like a Frisbee,' laughed the floppy haired boy, and with that he threw it as far as he could into the bushes. I wondered, as I chased after it, if the ball could

48

tell a story of family picnics or children's games and imagined scenes of laughter, sunshine and lemonade.

'Leave it, Rolo!' the floppy haired boy shouted as I scrambled through the undergrowth after the flat ball. He thought I wanted to play, but my intention was to tuck it away for safe keeping. I had a funny feeling about that ball.

'LEAVE!' he shouted a bit more urgently and I hid it under the bushes and made a great show of kicking up the leaves and twigs to bury it.

'Come, Rolo, let's go home,' and off we went. The floppy haired boy had lost interest.

That night, when the house was quiet, I heard a familiar tap-tapping on the kitchen window. Standing up and stretching I disentangled myself from my blanket and could make out the anxious faces of Yulia and Bubo the owl peering in through the glass, illuminated in the light of a tiny lantern.

I tiptoed across the kitchen tiles towards the sink, opened the trapdoor with my teeth and poked my head out into the night air.

'Athelstan needs you, Paddy Paws, come now!' and without further ado off we went through the forest. I was trotting the familiar path and Yulia was riding Bubo who flew low above my head.

We reached the dragon tree and Yulia alighted and whispered something to the owl who swooped off at once into the night.

'Ah, Little Pup, there is something important I need you to do. I want to send you to the Western Front in Northern France on Christmas Eve 1914. Are you game?' Athelstan spoke solemnly.

I was all ears. 1914? Surely that was at the beginning of the First World War. This could be dangerous, but I trusted Athelstan and the urgency of the mission.

'What do I need to do?' I asked the guardian of the

time tunnel.

'Gather the object you hid in the forest,' and without another word he faded into the bark as was his way.

'I'll never find that deflated ball in the dark!' I exclaimed to Yulia and right on cue a heavyish flat object landed on my head and bounced off. I spun around angrily. Bubo flew away hooting with laughter having delivered the missile on target.

'Athelstan had already briefed us and Bubo fetched the thing so we are ready to go,' Yulia smiled. I picked the flat ball up in my teeth and we approached the time tunnel. Yulia went in and the entrance shut rather abruptly behind her.

I coughed politely with the deflated ball still in my mouth. The door remained obstinately shut.

'Silly Paddy Paws, you forgot the orb!' said Yulia as the door reopened; she emerged and bent down to retrieve the small pink ball from its hiding place among the roots. She placed it in front of my paws and went into the tunnel again. The door closed. I kicked the pink ball with my front left paw – David Beckham style – and the orb rolled towards the entrance and the time tunnel yawned open to admit me. If the door could smirk I bet that's what it was doing right now.

'Into the time tunnel you go. Da, are you coming?' I heard grumbling and muttering and another lantern appeared and entered the tree and off we went on an adventure just over one hundred years back in time and along a few of miles beneath the English Channel – long before the Channel Tunnel of course – to the dangers of war-torn Northern France.

Emerging into a muddy field, I marked the entrance and waved off the woodland folk putting my nose up to sniff the air. A shell whizzed over my head and I ducked. I heard a voice shout,

'Hey, doggo, I don't know where you've come from

but you'd better get in here smartish or you'll be blown to kingdom come!'

I dropped the flattened ball in the mud and didn't wait for a second invitation. I launched myself into the deep trench from where the friendly voice had come and was immediately swept into the arms of a burly soldier whose green great coat smelt damp and musty. I buried my head inside his coat as he stroked me and I could smell raw tobacco.

'Jimmy, look what I've found wandering in no man's land. He must be a French mutt.'

'Parlez-vous anglais, petit chien?' the soldier said in my ear as he fussed it.

Yes, well, I can speak a bit of French as you know from my Montgolfier ballooning adventure, and I opened my mouth to reply but no words came out, only a bark, and anyway I doubted the soldiers would be able to hear me over the din of the shellfire being exchanged in the sky above our heads. It's funny how I can speak human on some time traveling adventures and not others.

'Steady on little fella,' my English rescuer hugged me tighter.

I peered down over the crook of his arm to the ground and noticed thick mud and puddles underfoot. I hoped he wasn't going to put me down. The war had only been raging for a few months but the bad weather had been relentless. These soldiers looked exhausted, dirty and demoralised – they had truly expected the war to be coming to an end by now so that they would be home by Christmas.

Here they were huddled against the sides of the trenches, raised slightly off the ground by wooden duckboards in an attempt to escape the permeating mud and damp. I expected the German soldiers in their trench just a few hundred yards away must feel the same. Conditions were appalling.

'Careful, Tom, he might be a German spy!' called another voice. I put what I hoped was an indignant expression on my face and licked Tom under his chin. I was surprised to find he was clean shaven – I thought the soldiers would be all bearded with little in the way of bathroom facilities in the trenches, but over his shoulder I spied a small cracked mirror propped up above a bowl of water perched on a tripod and a strop for sharpening cut throat razors. One of the men was shaving his face with lathered soap with his sleeves rolled up and his braces, which would normally be holding up his britches, dangling by his legs. The bottoms of his trousers were tied with string, to keep something out I imagined. I couldn't think what.

The soldier called Tom laughed and the other soldiers crowded round to make a fuss of me. I was pleased to bring smiles to these war-weary faces. Someone put a tin hat on my head and Tom said I could be their mascot and that they would call me Lucky.

Tom lifted me up and I put my paws on the top of the trench for a better look at the battlefield.

55

I couldn't really fathom why these nations were fighting to take possession of a few more yards of muddy field in a country that wasn't even theirs, but then I didn't understand the bigger picture either. 'Would you Adam and Eve it!' Tom called down to his companions, 'Fritz is putting up little Christmas trees like decorations and look, they're lighting candles!'

The men poked their heads up to see.

'Well it is Christmas Eve. I wonder what my Maud will be doing back in Blighty this evening...' said another. The soldiers fell silent, probably thinking about their sweethearts, wives and children back home.

'Hey up, lads, it's quiet time,' said a northern accent to my left. I looked across at the opposing trench and saw a placard being raised. All firing ceased and to my surprise, the Germans started calling out to the British and they exchanged friendly banter.

Tom organised a couple of men to climb out from the trench and go and retrieve their wounded where they lay fallen on the battle ground between the opposing trenches known as 'no man's land' and I saw the Germans do the same. The stretcher bearers wore white armbands with red crosses on.

The Germans threw something towards our trench and everyone ducked holding their tin hats firmly on their heads as they bobbed down below the parapet. Tom pulled me down with him.
To the amazement of the soldiers I jumped out to retrieve the missile.

It was a small package wrapped in a white handkerchief and tied with rough string. Not a grenade after all. Jimmy untied it.

'Chocolate!' Everyone gasped and Tom poked his head up above the trench,

'Danke, Fritz!' he shouted across the gloom, waving the bar at the gift-givers and to his men he added, 'there's enough for a square each – Happy Christmas everyone,' and he broke the chocolate bar into pieces and shared it out.

'Here, Jimmy, give us your smokes,' he addressed his chum.

Jimmy obliged by pulling out his army ration soft packet of Woodbine cigarettes from his breast pocket.

'Now then, Lucky, take these over to Fritz and make sure he doesn't keep you – be sure to come back, you're our mascot!'

I took the cigarette packet in my mouth and was lifted up over the top of the trench. I ran towards the Christmas tree line with its twinkling candles and was welcomed by young men speaking a language I knew to be German but didn't understand. These soldiers called me 'hund' and lifted me down, made a fuss of me and took the gifted cigarette packet. They were all young men far away from home and thoroughly fed up, just the same as the English across the muddy divide.

'Thank you, Tommy!' shouted a soldier with a twirly moustache in the direction of the British trench and he slipped me a piece of dried meat. It didn't touch the sides. No idea what meat it was. One of the German soldiers brought a small festive wreath made from twisted fir tree branches and decorated with ribbon. He hung it around my neck and they lifted me out from their trench and sent me back across no man's land to the other side. I kept my head down and couldn't see much, but I followed the direction of voices as the English soldiers whistled and called me.

It struck me how cold and frosty it was that night, which was probably a relief to the armies – respite from the endless rain.

A large moon rose, illuminating the field. No man's land looked like a giant football pitch.

Suddenly I had an idea. Still wearing the garland, I trotted over to where I had dropped the flattened ball. I picked it up with my teeth and ran back to the arms of Tom in the English trench.

The soldiers removed the wreath from my head and hung it on a stick visible from the other side and shouted across their appreciation for the gift.

'What have you got in your mouth Lucky?' Jimmy noticed the object I was carrying.

'Anyone got a bicycle pump?' he asked, flattening out the deflated ball.

The ball was passed down the line and miraculously

came back inflated, prompting the glimmer of a
smile to appear on the faces of the weary soldiers.

'Hey, Fritz – you play football?' Jimmy threw the ball
over the top and jumped out after it.

The German with the twirly moustache climbed out
from his trench with his hands turned down and his
arms spread wide to show he carried no weapons.

English and German soldiers followed their lead and
cautiously started climbing out from their trenches
and meeting in the middle, lining up and facing
each other. There were about eleven a side. Looked
like we had a game on!

I was anxious to join in and ran around barking my encouragement. It was good to see these men forget their hostilities and enjoy a little Christmas recreation, even if it was only a temporary reprieve from the horrors of war.

The game ended 4–1 to England and it was all very good natured. The soldiers shook hands and wished each other 'Merry Christmas' in their own languages as they returned to the cold comfort – I won't say safety – of their sodden trenches.

NOW I knew why Athelstan had sent me.
I was drifting off to sleep, snuggled up inside Tom's greatcoat listening to his strong heartbeat while the soldiers played cards.

I thought I must be imaging things. I could hear music drifting across no man's land – it appeared to be coming from the German trench. The soldiers were singing 'Stille Nacht', their version of Silent Night, and tuneful voices rose, filling the unusual silence of the temporary truce.

When the last notes had been sung the English soldiers applauded. Then Tom's solid bass voice sang the opening words of 'The First Noel' and others joined in. The Germans applauded afterwards and then sang 'Oh Tannenbaum' about the Christmas tree as it was their turn again.

Jimmy reminded his comrades that the idea of having a Christmas tree in the house originally came from Germany – it was Prince Albert's initiative when he married Queen Victoria.

When Tom broke into 'Oh Come All Ye Faithful' the Germans joined in, singing the Latin words 'Adeste Fidelis'. The two languages blended harmoniously from this extraordinary impromptu Anglo–German male voice choir and the sound rang out filling the eerie silence of that cold frosty Christmas Eve. This was something I would never ever forget. There wasn't a dry eye in the trenches. Those battle-weary young soldiers were homesick and war sick.

Time for me to slip away; I left the English soldiers

reminiscing about loved ones at home, Christmases past and sharing stories. I'm sure the Germans were doing exactly the same.

I glanced at the football lying in the middle of no man's land and wondered if it would ever be used again.

A sudden flash illuminating the sky overhead had me nervously looking up, thinking that hostilities had resumed. There was no accompanying sound however, just occasional flashes of what seemed like fire overhead. Soldiers in both trenches were scratching their heads and holding up their hands 'it's not us chum, the truce holds until tomorrow.' Suddenly I realised what it was – not gunfire at all but those pesky dragons Reod and Alba sparring away again high up in the sky!

I wondered if the soldiers could see the dragons and, if they could, what they would make of it all. They would probably think they were hallucinating.

'Did you do any good?' asked Yulia holding up her lantern to show me the way into the tunnel. 'You are very muddy indeed!'

I told her about the football match and the singing and then added that I wished I could have warned all those young men about the dangers to their health of smoking. Yulia smiled. It would be almost a hundred years before mankind worked that one out.

'Anyway, not many of those young men returned from The Great War,' she remarked soberly.

Talking to Athelstan about my experience he told me that the Christmas Truce of 1914 was never repeated.

'The Allied troops were ordered by High Command to cease at once any kind of fraternising with the enemy - it was considered an offence punishable by Court Martial. And, as it happens,' Athelstan continued, 'other nationalities that fought alongside the British in the trenches were angered by the Christmas truce too and could not understand how you could break off from fighting a war, enjoy some recreation time with the enemy and then resume killing each other.'

I knew I had witnessed a very special moment in history.

Weary with exhaustion and forgetting all that Yulia had said about being muddy, I crept back to my basket where I sank into a deep sleep.

A couple of hours later the kitchen door opened. 'Rolo! What on earth have you been up to?' said the smiley lady with her hands on her hips. 'Obviously my lazy boy only tickled you with the brush after your forest walk yesterday afternoon, if he used it at all!'

As I went out into the back garden I could hear the taps running and the brisk swishing of shampoo in the utility room sink. I could tell I was in for a bath.

Rolodogblog #2 #thedrone

The smiley lady was using delaying
tactics for our walk this morning.
When we finally got out, she marched
me straight over to the field and
I was delighted to see that my
great friends Merlin and Juno were
already there. We had a great game
of 'I wee, you wee,' and chased
Merlin's tennis ball for ages. That
big dog is far too polite to snatch
his ball off me, and Juno and I both
have terrier skills so we sneaked
his much-loved tennis ball away
and ran around like this for ages,
wearing each other out (which is
actually impossible for a terrier).
The humans usually get bored before
we run out of energy.

A man appeared with a large camera
on a tripod, microphone and an

interesting looking bag. He introduced himself to the smiley lady and the other dog owners as a reporter for a national television company.

I listened in to this 'breaking news': the residents of College Fields want to adopt the open space as 'Town Green' which means it can't be built on but freely used by anyone for recreational purposes. There is an objection to this by a party who declined to be interviewed. They were saying it was something to do with an access road and a plan to build new houses on an agricultural field beyond.

Everyone was invited to have their say on camera. There was no holding back and the smiley lady and I both said our piece.

The reporter filmed us dogs playing and our people chatting and it was a glorious sunny morning. All was going well.

Then the reporter opened the black bag and took out a strange black object. He flicked a switch and it started making a loud bleeping sound and it took to the air. This reminded me of an incident with the floppy haired boy's helicopter — I had once tried to 'kill' that because the noise it made nearly drove me mad. This thing was making the same sound.

I still had Merlin's tennis ball in my mouth and I wasn't going to drop that, so I couldn't bark at the bleeping thing at first but I kept running round in circles as it rose up in the sky and hovered

menacingly overhead. I dropped
the ball and started barking and
jumping up at it. It soared higher
and I could hear the reporter
saying,

'I'm getting great aerial footage,
keep up the chatter everyone,
there's a good dog, well done
Rolo.'

When the man felt he'd filmed enough
action for the news story he wanted
to land the whirring craft. I was
having none of it.

The smiley lady was spinning round
the cameraman trying to get hold
of my harness to clip my lead back
on. I wasn't going to let her stop
me — I couldn't understand why the
bleeping didn't affect the humans in
the same way it got to me.

She shouted to the cameraman 'keep the drone up until I get hold of Rolo or he'll destroy it!'

The other dog owners joined in the chase — everyone was trying to catch hold of me whilst the annoying thing beeped on overhead. Merlin and Juno sat on the grass watching me with what I can only assume was admiration. Couldn't they hear it?

71

Eventually I was rugby tackled to the ground and put on my lead and led swiftly away from the scene. As the reporter packed away the now sleeping bleeping thing I hear him mutter 'Note to self; never work with Jack Russell's.'

At last the thing was safely back in its bag. This reminded me of a similar incident when the smiley lady's smoke alarm went off. It kept on beeping and flashing and she had to climb up a step ladder and take it down from the hall ceiling. She put the offending object on top of the dresser saying something about a replacement battery and was very angry with me indeed when I managed to get it down and kill it. It didn't beep any more.

#rolosavestheday

Chapter 4

Rolo and King Alfred the Great

'Mum, why was King Alfred called 'Alfred the Great' and not 'Alfred the First'?' asked the floppy haired boy.

The smiley lady put a plateful of steaming shepherd's pie in front of him and took off her oven gloves. 'Good point. I've never thought about it. I have no idea.' She answered truthfully. 'Why don't you research it?'

I was sitting very quietly under the table with my feet gathered beneath me, doing what they both call 'clown eyes' hoping to get a spoonful of that shepherd's pie.

The smiley lady went to the sink and filled the empty dish with soapy water. She must have seen me looking a bit crestfallen as she then winked at me. She'd already put some in my doggy bowl to cool down and now placed this on the floor in front of me.

73

After we had finished dinner there was a delicious aroma of freshly baked Welsh cakes coming from the kitchen. I watched the smiley lady roll the dough and use a glass to cut small circles out and then fry the second batch in hot butter on a griddle. Every now and then a bit of dough would fall on the floor. I feel I earn my keep by being the canine vacuum cleaner. The kitchen floor is always spotless.

'All I remember about King Alfred is that he was supposed to have burned the cakes,' the smiley lady said.

That night I took myself off to the forest to ask Athelstan, as he seems to know everything about history.

'What do you know about King Alfred? What was so 'great' about him?' I asked.

'Well now, Little Pup, where to begin? He kept his kingdom of Wessex safe from the invading Vikings during his reign from 871 to 899; he changed the

way the Anglo Saxons fought which helped defeat
the enemy, and he unified the Saxons for the first
time. Is that a good enough reason?' replied the sage
dragon.

'Did he burn the cakes?' I pressed.

'Well now, I think a trip to 9th century Wessex is
in order. Instead of going through the time tunnel,
Rhydian will take you, and perhaps Gwyn as well.
It's time he tested his wings, under supervision of
course.'

It struck me that wise as the tree dragon was, he
perhaps wasn't aware of Gwyn's solo adventure
ending up in a red kite's nest.

'Stand back! Incoming dragon!' Athelstan roared
and instinctively I ducked between the oak tree
roots unsure of what was going to happen next.
There was a great whooshing followed by a flapping
of powerful wings and Rhydian the Welsh dragon
landed deftly in front of the tree where I had just

been standing. If I had stayed there I would have been squashed!

'Noswaith dda, Athelstan,' Rhydian boomed in greeting in his gruff Welsh language and turning to me, gave a slight bow and said 'Ci Em', which I remembered meant 'Jewel Dog'.

Formalities over, Rhydian the great red dragon lay down flat on the forest floor and put his mighty tail out behind him like a drawbridge. I needed no second invitation: I went round to his tail end and ran up it like a ramp. This was much easier than trying to scramble onto the dragon's back from the bank of a ditch like I had last time I went for a dragon ride. I climbed over his rough scales up to his neck and tried to get comfy. The scales were hard and prickly but I wasn't one to complain.

'Wait for us!' I heard the tinkling voice of Yulia and was amazed to see her perched on Gwyn's back, holding her lantern high and steering him with small reins gathered in one hand. The woodland girl's face was a picture of concentration as they swooped in low through the trees to join us.

'Whoa!' she soothed, pulling on the reins.
They came in to land in a much more ungainly fashion than the red dragon. Yulia did well to keep her seat.

'Roro!' burbled Gwyn. I think he was pleased to see me.

'We need to work on your landing skills a bit,' said Yulia, repositioning herself on the young white dragon's back. I could see he was just the right size for her to ride – he certainly wasn't ready to take the weight of anything bigger yet.

'How are we going to go back in history if we are not using the tunnel?' I asked. I knew I'd travelled back to the Iron Age by dragon before but I couldn't remember how we'd done it.

'Wait and see,' said Athelstan with his customary mysteriousness.

Well that told me. I waited and watched. We bade farewell to the amused tree dragon.

'What do you know about King Alfred?' I asked Yulia when we were both airborne astride our dragons and clear of the trees.

'Only what Athelstan has told me; he was the youngest of five sons and probably never expected to rule. By all accounts Alfred was very religious and possibly destined for the church. Three of his brothers died. His ruling brother Aethelred of Wessex was having problems with 'The Great Heathen Army'.'

'Who were they?' I interrupted.

'The invading Vikings who came in long ships, plundered coastal towns, settled without too much opposition in York, which they called Jorvik, in East Anglia, Northumberland and Mercia and had their sights set on Wessex,' she explained. 'Alfred distinguished himself in battle by leading an army

The Secret Adventures of Rolo

on behalf of his brother, the king, although he disliked war himself.'

'What you might call a pacifist,' I mused, eager to contribute, 'but surely there was enough man power in Anglo Saxon England to see off the marauders?'

'The problem was, Paddy Paws,' Yulia continued, 'that in the 9th century Saxony was split into several kingdoms and each looked after their own. Most Saxon kings paid off the Vikings so they would leave their territories in peace and go and invade a neighbouring kingdom instead. The Vikings even managed to occupy some Saxon kingdoms and appointed 'puppet kings' to rule from among the locals. There was no leadership and no unity until Alfred came to rule following his brother Aethelred's death aged twenty-one.'

She broke off and leaned forward to speak into the white dragon's ear,

'Gwyn, you have to concentrate now. You've got to

get this bit right or we'll be left behind! Follow the red dragon!'

The young white dragon slowed his pace a fraction and tucked in behind Rhydian as instructed. What happened next I'm not too sure about as I felt a bit travel sick, but we seemed to ascend rapidly above the clouds and as we wove in and out we made a big figure of eight in the sky.

I glanced behind to see if Gwyn had kept up and sure enough the white dragon's expression was focused on this tricky manoeuvre. I looked in a forward direction again as I didn't want to throw up, and then when we reached the point of the figure of eight from where we had started, we suddenly swooped low underneath the cloud line.

I heard Yulia's voice call anxiously to her steed 'remember to dip your wings,' and sure enough we had done it – rolled back the centuries and two dragons and their riders touched down in 9th century Wessex.

The landing site was a bit boggy and when I disembarked I felt my paws sinking into mud. I wondered where we were exactly.

Rhydian answered my thought. He seemed to have the same mind-reading power that Athelstan had.

'Somerset Marshes, Ci Em,' he replied. 'In the year 878 if we've done this right.'

What would happen next, I wondered.

I could see armed men ranging about the marshes and, by the looks of their weapons and the style of their helmets, they were Saxons. They wore rounded helmets which came right round their faces covering their ears. The men carried wooden shields, axes, swords, spears and some had bows and arrows. There were no signs of any horses. This Wessex army was made up of foot soldiers, which meant a battle might resemble a giant rugby scrum with the addition of lots of shouting and lethal blows from their heavy weapons. The Saxons appeared to be big stocky men more used to ploughing a field than wielding a sword, but with plenty of muscle power between them.

Yulia and the dragons went to find somewhere to hide but I thought I'd hang around to get a better look.

One of the soldiers spotted me and I was immediately picked up by strong rough arms, fussed and carried into a hut where I was placed at the feet of none other than Alfred, the King of Wessex himself.

My first impression was that the king didn't look too great: pale, thin and he kept clutching his stomach – he seemed to be in a lot of pain. I wondered if Yulia might be able to help him. She's good with healing herbs and nature and suchlike. I wondered if I could fetch her. The king was praying a lot and pacing around the room, completely ignoring me. I noticed a woman kneading dough on the wooden table close by. Flour was flying everywhere as she worked little balls of the mixture and flattened them with her hand. She was working at great speed. I wondered if they were Welsh cakes like the smiley lady makes. Or perhaps more accurately these would be Wessex cakes.

'Leave me now. I need to think,' the king spoke gruffly.

'But, sire, I have just put these cakes in the oven,' the woman protested.

The soldier who had brought me indoors said,

'Hush, Hilde, the king will see to the cakes, won't you, sire? Let's leave him be.' And with that the pair left the dwelling without a backward glance.

Alfred lay down on a pallet of straw and clutched his stomach. I jumped up beside him and snuggled in like I do when the floppy haired boy doesn't feel well.

The king's frown turned to a weak smile and I found we could converse. He didn't seem surprised by this.

'You seem troubled, sire. Is it the impending battle?' I asked.

The king shared his thoughts with me,

'The problem with the Vikings is that they are stealthy, like thieves in the night. They come in their long ships and land on our coasts, plunder our villages and when they move across the land they move quickly, like lightning. They are unstoppable, motivated by greed and love of treasure; they are even settling on our beloved land! I can't keep calling the men away from the fields they tend every time there is a raid, and I can't afford to keep a standing army. But I will not have the Vikings settle here in Wessex. What to do?' he pondered.

'Well, why don't you engage half the men to fight with you when necessary and leave half at home to tend the crops? That way you have a regular army ready to muster at once should the need arise.'

The king looked at me with astonishment.

'That's a brilliant idea; I'll create an army mobilised from freemen to defend their shire. It will be called a 'fyrd'. Well done… what's your name?'

'Rolo,' I answered.

'I shall make you a theyn, Rodor.'

Rodor? And what's a 'theyn'? Some kind of cake perhaps? I hoped so, but it felt impolite to ask. Instead I said,

'Why do you call me Rodor?'

'Because you came from the sky. And because of your wisdom I shall make you one of my noblemen.'

Aha, so that's what a theyn was.

85

Well, if Alfred saw me arrive from the air, he must have seen the dragons too. And then, as though reading my thoughts, the king said,

'We have a red and a white dragon around here – are they the two that brought you to me? Are you a gift from the dragons?'

This news was astonishing. Dragons here too! I wasn't quite sure how to respond so I just crossed my paws and did 'clown eyes'.

'I have a plan for keeping our realm safe from invaders, but I've not told anyone yet,' he said and went on to explain to me his theory about 'burhs'. 'My plan is to make garrisons in every town in Wessex.'

'What does that mean?' I interrupted.

'Fortifying the market places, and men will be given plots of land in exchange for their muscle power, defending the town in time of war. If I can create these 'burhs' in key places, then neighbouring villages will also come under the protection of their nearest 'burh' and we will have a realistic and strong network of defence against the Vikings, whenever they dare to plunder. I will also use this 'fyrd' system of half army, half labourer in time of battle as we have just discussed.

'And I have another plan hatching in my mind: I shall keep a written record of the size of each town, the number of men required to maintain its defence and the length of the ramparts needed and so forth,' he paused.

'A sort of blueprint for each town within the kingdom?' I encouraged.

'Yes, Rodor, exactly that. This will help future kings with their planning. I have started this experiment already, spreading out from my palace in Winchester to neighbouring towns, and I intend to take the defence plan around the kingdom and even to adjoining ones if it is successful. I've heard a rumour that even our old enemy the Welsh want an alliance with me! That would certainly give this land greater power. Come what may, we will defeat these Vikings! I have such long term plans…' The king's face crumpled with pain and he stopped tickling my ears to clutch at his stomach again.

'I came here with someone who might be able to help you, sire,' I said and explained about Yulia with her knowledge of nature.

The king nodded his consent and I bounded out from the dwelling towards the woods, watching out for roaming Vikings.

'What's the rush, Paddy Paws? We've just spotted some pesky dragons fighting overhead. Rhydian wants to have a word with them,' said Yulia when I found her in the trees.

I explained about the king's discomfort and the woodland girl, instructing Rhydian to keep a close eye on Gwyn, immediately started foraging for herbs: comfrey, borage and some others I'd never heard of and didn't know what they looked like so I couldn't be of much help. I ran around the woods following the scent of deer and rabbits and marking the trees. I saw Yulia with a bunch of greenery in her arms and watched her speak further with Rhydian. I showed her the king's dwelling. Yulia entered clutching the leaves and immediately wrinkled her nose at the terrible smell of burning.

The king jumped up, 'I forgot all about the wretched cakes!'

He wrapped his royal hands in his cloak and quickly removed the smoking tray from the top of the open fire and threw the charred offerings down on the table. They flew off the tray. Even I would turn my nose up at burnt cakes. I didn't think Hilde would be too pleased.

'Right, let's sort you out first, sire, and then we'll see about the cakes.' Yulia immediately took charge. The woodland girl scurried around the crude Saxon

kitchen and was soon chopping and then pounding
the herbs with a flint pestle and mortar she found
on a shelf, adding water from a pitcher to make a
drinkable potion. It was green and looked like it had
come from the bottom of a pond. Rather him than
me.

King Alfred grimaced and Yulia pinched his nose
and told him to drink it down like a good boy. He
obeyed the bossy girl and soon fell into a deep sleep
and by the look on his face was temporarily free of
pain.

Yulia set about making another batch of cakes,

whirling round the kitchen and gathering up the ingredients which had been left out by Hilde's rapid departure.

The woodland girl assured me as she baked that the king would recover his health and go on to do many great things. Famously, he would initiate the translation of important texts from Latin into Old English to make them accessible to his men, thus helping to improve their minds so they could live worthy and informed lives.

'This Christian king will unite the Saxons and lay the foundations of a code of law,' Yulia continued. This I believed because of the passion with which Alfred spoke.

Yulia picked up the skillet, filled it with flattened dough circles and put it on the grate over the fire.

'Athelstan told me that during parleys with the enemy Alfred had great success converting pagan leaders to Christianity and sometimes even stood as godfather to their children when he baptised them,' Yulia added, 'but of course all of this is in his future.'

I was beginning to understand Alfred's greatness. Hopefully sleep would ease the king's pain and help clear his mind.

Yulia had just retrieved the new batch of cakes when Hilde came through the door with a rabbit for the royal dinner. She put the rabbit on the flour-covered table ready to skin and stew, smiled approvingly at the warm cakes and went over to check on the sleeping king. His face had taken on a rosy hue. We bundled up the burnt cakes in a cloth and scarpered. She didn't take any notice of us.

We made for the woods in search of Rhydian and Gwyn.

Overhead there was an almighty din. I looked up and saw four dragons, two red and two white, one a fair bit smaller than the others and trailing tiny reins. The dragons seemed to be having a great

game of air tag, swooping low and flying up high,
breathing fire and mock fighting.

93

'What are they up to?' I asked Yulia.

'Well I had suggested that they put on a bit of a pantomime to scare off the invaders,' she said.

It seemed to be working – the Vikings were fleeing! We watched big burly men with plaited beards and ponytails poking out from their pointed helmets, waving long swords and running for the hills screaming like banshees.

The dragons came down to land in a clearing away from the hut and out of sight from the Wessex men who were rubbing their hands with glee. They had won this battle without too much fighting and no loss of life; although to hear them talk you would think they had won this skirmish on their own merit without the help of the dragons.

'Those Vikings will be half way back to their base at Chippenham by now,' I heard one say, 'but no doubt they will be back.'

The dragons were breathless and chuckling; boasting about their abilities to scare men and turn a battle. They were also ravenously hungry.

Yulia threw the burnt cakes on the ground and all four set upon them as if they hadn't eaten for a week.

∾∾∾

Relaying the story of our adventure to Athelstan he enlightened me that Alfred's 'burhs' evolved into what we now know today as 'boroughs' and that most of the garrisoned towns eventually became the county towns of England. I also learned that Alfred was a strategist, thinking beyond his own borders and in his twenty-eight year reign he successfully unified the different kingdoms into a more efficient Anglo Saxon England. Most importantly he halted the Viking advance. Alfred's legacy was truly great and I was lucky to have been able to witness this first hand.

'Did you find out any more about King Alfred?' asked the smiley lady when the floppy haired boy came home from school the next day.

'Well, he was local,' the floppy haired boy replied throwing down his bag in the hallway. 'Born in Wantage and died in Winchester. Apparently there weren't any burnt cakes – that's just a story,' he added.

There are times when I really wish I could speak to my humans.

Rolodogblog #3 #petservice

The smiley lady is an assistant church warden. It sounds very grand, but what it really means, I think, is she sometimes puts up the hymn numbers on a big board before the Sunday service. I'm only guessing what the role entails as I'm only allowed to go to church with her when it's the annual pet service.

This is a wonderful event because

about twenty dogs of all breeds, shapes and sizes get together in the churchyard, sing a few hymns and are blessed and go home with a doggy bag of yummy treats. I like being a holy dog. My name goes on the rota as warden for that service, not the smiley lady.

On this particular Sunday Pet Service it was raining. The smiley lady was panicking because it's better to have the pet service outside rather than having everyone indoors. Luckily the rain soon stopped, the people tipped the puddles off the plastic chairs and I settled down to watch the canine congregation arriving.

The usual suspects were there: a pair of spaniels, Tia an elderly sheepdog, another Jack Russell

called Suzy, Sparkle a terrier
(who doesn't like me very much)
and Maisie the corgi. We all
settled down under the chairs, paws
together, eyes closed.

As the service began, all eyes
opened wide and collectively
focused on a late arrival. A family
were carrying a cage between them,
making their way down the gravel
path from the car park. We were all
eager to know what was inside. It
was a slow and careful walk.

The inhabitant of the cage was
shrouded like a budgie and remained
very quiet throughout the service.
We didn't get to find out what it
was despite lots of sniffing and
whining and straining at our leads
especially during 'All things
bright and beautiful'.

The service ended without incident and everyone started to stack their chairs saying how enjoyable the half hour had been and why didn't we do this more often than once a year. The vicar rolled her eyes and scurried quickly inside the church.

I was being taken home by a neighbour because the smiley lady had to stay behind and do wardenly things in the vestry, whatever they were.

She told the story to the floppy haired boy over Sunday lunch, 'Someone came into the vestry and told us that one of the attending dogs had come back to see what was in the cage... only it wasn't in the cage: the rabbit was sat on the children's laps being petted after they thought all the dogs

had gone home. It seems that a
small white black and brown terrier
appeared from nowhere, off the lead
and making straight for the happy
scene, followed in hot pursuit by
a red faced and breathless man
brandishing a lead and shouting
"Get that rabbit in its cage —
there's a Jack Russell on the
loose!"

The smiley lady said she had
laughed rather smugly once she knew
the rabbit had been safely rehoused
and taken home with no harm done.
She was thinking it couldn't have
been Yours Truly because I'd

already been taken home. I'll let
you decide for yourselves whether
the naughty dog was me or one of
the others…

#rololovesrabbits

Rolodogblog #4 #Dubai

The smiley lady visits Dubai in the
United Arab Emirates a couple of
times a year. She spent 20 years
living there and still has a lot of
friends in that place. I've heard
her saying many times that it's
changed a lot over the years.

I know, from various conversations,
that there is another family dog.
He is called Leo and is a desert
dog, whatever that is. He came from
a rescue place just like me. He is
a very grand old man of 14 and I've

seen him and heard him through a magical device on the computer — I believe it's called Skype.

I always know when the smiley lady is going to Dubai on holiday because she gets her suitcase out and packs summer clothes, a sun hat, high factor sun screen, sunglasses and sandals. Apparently it's very hot out there most of the year, as it is a city built in the desert.

Well, I'd like to go there and I sometimes imagine what it would be like to sneak onto the big airplane for a journey that takes 7 hours with food and television provided in the comfy seats. What fun I'd have meeting Leo and visiting the water parks, beach and souk and the tallest building in the world, all places I've heard the floppy haired boy talk about.

I mentioned this to Athelstan in conversation, wondering what the tree dragon might know about this popular and fast evolving Emirate, which is a principality in the Middle East. He didn't disappoint me.

'Would you like to see for yourself, Little Pup? The time tunnel can get you there quicker than any modern airline and you won't even need a passport! I can send you to meet the man who became the first President of the UAE back in 1971 — he likes dogs!'

#rololovesdubai

Chapter 5

Rolo and the founding of the United Arab Emirates

On my way through the time tunnel and not really knowing what to expect on this adventure, I asked Yulia if she knew anything of the history of the area. 'Archaeology has revealed that this desert region shows signs of habitation going back to at least 3000BC,' the woodland girl told me as she held up her lantern to light the way.

'But the United Arab Emirates, or UAE as it is known today, has only existed a short time, less than 50 years. Prior to that it was desert populated by Bedouin tribes: nomads who divided their time between the ocean, for fishing and pearl diving; the desert, for rearing camels and herds; and the oasis, for cultivating dates and growing vegetables.'

'What does Bedouin mean?' I asked.

'Desert dweller. They were resourceful and independent tribesmen famed for their tradition of offering hospitality to guests.'

Goody – sounds like there will be food. I didn't know much about the history of the UAE except I'd heard the floppy haired boy saying that its sudden wealth came from the discovery of oil in the 1950s. 'Athelstan said that it was a timely discovery because the region was having a hard time after the loss of revenue from pearl diving due to the invention of the Japanese cultured pearl. When oil was discovered no one knew at first how much there would be or how long oil revenue might last and so oil exportation only began in the early 1960's,' Yulia continued, 'and that turned Abu Dhabi from being one of the poorest sheikdoms into the richest.

'Who was the ruler?' I asked.

'Sheikh Zayed Bin Sultan al Nahyan became Ruler of Abu Dhabi in 1966. He had the foresight to reinvest money from oil sales so the industry began to flourish and the wealth of the Trucial States grew, with the sheikhdom of Dubai under the Maktoum family expanding its reputation of being the region's leading trading post.' Golly, Yulia knew her Middle East history!

I came out from the time tunnel in a warm dry and sandy place. It was already dusk but the sand retained warmth from the heat of the sun. All I could see around me was desert. The temperature reminded me of my visit to Ancient Egypt in the time of the Pharaohs.

Yulia waved me off and told me to drink plenty of water in this climate. I could feel the temperature creep down as night rolled its inky blanket over the vast sky.

I looked up and noticed at once how starry it was and then cocked my ear as I heard a sound and instinctively lay low. Two fleet-footed dogs ran past me and then came back for a sniff and a look.

'As-Salaam-Alaikum,' said one.

The other bowed in my direction.

'Hello, I'm Rolo,' I replied, hoping they could understand me. They looked a bit like greyhounds, sleek and noble. They seemed amused by my appearance.

'Our master will like to meet you, he likes little dogs and needs some distraction, come with us!' in heavily accented English, and with that they ran full pelt across the dunes and I had no choice but to follow, struggling to keep up, my little legs going nineteen to the dozen. I followed the long-legged dogs, who were chatting away with ease whilst they ran, telling me about their breed called Saluki, a kind of greyhound formerly used for hunting and now the preferred breed of Arab sheikhs.

We approached a simply dressed man sitting cross-legged in the sand. His head was covered with a cloth and he wore a loose white gown and sandals. Close by stood a fine white Arab horse with its reins hanging loose, and on a post was a falcon, hooded and tethered by a jess around its foot.

The horse whickered softly as the dogs approached and the man looked up. He had a kindly face and dark brown eyes. This was the ruler of Abu Dhabi.

'As-Salaam-Alaikum,' he greeted me with the same pleasant sounding words that the salukis had used.

'Noor, Rayaan, who is this little fellow?'

108

I bowed deeply and told him my name. He held out his hand inviting me to approach, so I snuggled beside him on the sand, near a small fire. The man smelt nice – sort of perfumed. He ruffled my ears and together we enjoyed the peace and solitude of the desert sky at night. The salukis stretched out at his feet. Luckily he spoke in perfect English,

'My forefathers used the stars to guide them through life, whether it be across the desert by camel, to navigate at sea, to help whilst fishing or even to tell when the weather was going to change. With all the modern technology in the 20th century, we still use the stars, and I find comfort and peace in the desert at night away from artificial light,' he mused, continuing to stroke my ears.

'Tomorrow is a monumental day, but I cannot sleep. I have come out here to be at peace and to think. I am going to meet with my brothers from the Bani Yas tribal confederation and we are going to formalise the treaty of the United Arab Emirates; they have chosen me to be first President'. He sighed heavily with the responsibility and looked at me.

'It's a great honour and all have put their trust in me to unite our brothers.'

The fire crackled in approval.

'Our original plan had been to join with Bahrain and Kuwait and our seven sheikhdoms, in accordance with the treaty of the 1820s brokered by the British to keep this area of the Gulf at peace, but Bahrain and Kuwait have since been granted independence of their own. However, even without them we will prove stronger together. You are a British dog are you not? They are very shrewd people. They want to keep friendly with us so as to keep their trade links with India secure. The British have spent a lot of time and naval power keeping other Europeans away over the years,' he laughed.

'They announced their intention to withdraw from the region three years ago and finally we will rule ourselves. Tomorrow, 2nd December, is the appointed date. Have you come to witness the signing?'

I nodded and snuggled in closer. I suppose I had, although not in an official capacity.

'The ruling sheikhs of Dubai, Sharjah, Ajman, Umm al Quwain and Fujeirah are all coming to sign this treaty at the Guest Palace in Dubai right on the sea shore.'

'Wait, you've forgotten one, what about Ras al Khaimah?' I asked, eager to show off my knowledge of the UAE learned from the floppy haired boy.

'No, they are not coming. We are still in negotiation with them,' Sheikh Zayed stroked his beard thoughtfully.

'I have such big plans for this region,' he said and his eyes lit up in the firelight as he talked to me of his dreams of expansion. 'Now all you see are fishing huts, Barasti, made from palm fronds and a few low-

111

rise buildings.' He took a stick and started drawing pictures in the sand.

'We are going to extend the creek by dredging it and by building a fine port here. This will become one of the biggest ports in the world. There will also be a dry dock for ship building and repairs. Dhows, built in the traditional way by hand riveted wooden pegs, will continue to ply their trade across the Persian Gulf to Iran, Pakistan and India and further around the Arabian Sea to Africa. The creek and port will play a very important part in the development of Dubai as a leading trade hub. Workers will come from all over. New airports in each emirate. Our own airline. We will be the envy of the world, you mark my words.'

No wonder he is remembered as a man of great vision.

A glow on the horizon in the east made us realise dawn was approaching fast. Sheikh Zayed unrolled a prayer mat and faced east, making salaams and repeating phrases. I waited respectfully some distance away. When he had finished he kicked sand over the dying embers of his campfire, rolled up his prayer mat and tied it behind the saddle, brushed the sand off his clothes, took up the falcon on his arm, mounted his horse, whistling his salukis to follow.

'Yalla, we must go. Come and see history being made,' he shouted back to me and without waiting for my reply, spurred his horse into a gallop. I ran with the salukis across the dunes, our paws leaving straight tracks behind us. Luckily we didn't have too far to travel.

We approached a simple marble building surrounded by big whitewashed walls and waited in the courtyard whilst Sheik Zayed was ushered inside to freshen up and change his kandora for the big ceremony. His horse and falcon were led away. I remembered Yulia's words and drank thirstily from a stone water trough. The salukis disappeared and I flopped out in the shade to watch the dignitaries arrive. Although it was early December and technically winter, the sun was warming things up nicely and I enjoyed the sensation of lying on a warm marble step.

After a doze, I peered through an open French door, past the long velvet curtain, and counted twenty-one people in the interestingly shaped round room which was dominated by a large circular wooden table with inlaid leather panels. So, this was where the signing was to take place.

A large chandelier was suspended from the ceiling in the centre of the domed room. The crystal pendants caught the light from the December sun and as they twinkled they reminded me of the starry Arabian sky I'd seen the previous night.

On the table lay many documents, pens and glasses of water. This was not the time to jump on the table and change the declaration like I had attempted with Magna Carta in England some 800 years previously! I overheard an Englishman called Sir Geoffrey

Arthur being introduced. He was there to sign on behalf of Her Britannic Majesty's government and he stood out because he was the only dignitary in a Western suit. The others wore what I assumed to be traditional Arab robes with their heads covered with white or red and white checked cloths. Everyone ignored me, even my new friend from last night. To be fair I think he was a bit busy.

After the signing of the declaration everyone left the room and assembled outside. There were photographers and reporters from all around the world. I thought it best if I kept out of sight. I had travelled almost fifty years back in time to witness this historic event; I wasn't supposed to be there so I didn't want to be photographed or appear on the BBC 6 o'clock news.

I was just thinking it was time to return to my own era when everyone's attention was drawn to an empty flagpole; the new red, green, white and black flag which symbolised Arab unity was about to be hoisted for the very first time. I had a running commentary from Rayaan who had reappeared by my side. I asked him questions about the traditional clothing and he explained that white robe was called a kandora and the head scarf was called a ghutrah, held in place with a rope called an igal which could be used in an emergency to hobble a straying camel. The saluki seemed to enjoy the limelight and wandered off to his master's side to be included in the historic photographs.

A twenty-one-gun salute was fired to signal the founding of the United Arab Emirates and the new flag was raised. I don't know what happened after that as I took off as fast as I could, as soon as the first shot was fired. You probably recall I don't like loud noises!

It was just as well I remembered the way out from the palace, though I wondered how I would ever find my way across the desert to the time tunnel entrance. Luckily I managed to retrace our footprints as there had been no 'shamal' or desert wind blowing sand to cover them.

Yulia's lantern shone out like a welcome beacon. What an exciting adventure! I had witnessed the founding of the United Arab Emirates! I'm only sorry that I didn't get to meet Leo – but I was about 35 years too early for him. I sincerely wished I could tell the floppy haired boy all about my adventure but he wouldn't have believed me even if I could have done. I suddenly felt homesick and tired and couldn't wait to get back to my basket.

'Paddy Paws, you're all covered in sand,' exclaimed Yulia.

'Yalla,' I practised my new word. Let's go.

Rolodogblog #5 #harvestfestival

I walked down to church with the smiley lady and the floppy haired boy. We left her there for the 10 o'clock harvest festival family service. I'd like to have seen inside the church because

apparently everyone brings food to
be distributed to those in need
at the food shelter afterwards.
Traditionally harvest gifts used
to be home grown produce from the
garden, allotment or farm: runner
beans, carrots, potatoes, homemade
jams and chutneys or freshly baked
bread in the shape of a sheath of
corn — but these days it tends to
be dry goods like pasta and rice
and tins of food bought from the
supermarket. I'd like to have seen
the display nonetheless.

The floppy haired boy and I
continued our walk along the
riverbank and the sound of the
organ playing and voices raised
singing 'we plough the fields and
scatter' grew fainter as we walked
further away from the church. I
was off the lead and my curiosity

got the better of me — it's now or never, I thought — and I bolted back without looking round at my young master, back along the footpath and straight to the big wooden door of the church. It was shut fast. I'm sure I could hear the smiley lady chirping away because I know it's her favourite childhood hymn and I was frustrated not to be able to go in and be with her and see all the food decorating the church. Never mind I'll just sit and wait for the door to open.

119

There were matching baskets of blackberries and apples used as decoration on either side of the stone porch. I tucked in, ate the little ripe blackberries right off their stalks and polished off the lovely juicy russet apples.

I had a pang of guilt and then decided these weren't destined for the needy and carried on scoffing. Just then a towering shadow filled the porch and I knew I was in trouble. Never mind ploughing the fields, I certainly scattered — the remaining blackberries and apple stalks all over the floor. The floppy haired boy's hand reached down to reattach the lead to my harness and he marched me home in silence.

The smiley lady heard the story later and for some reason she couldn't stop giggling. Blackberry and apple go well together I have to say, but where was the pastry? Where was the custard? #harvestfestival #blackberryandapplepie

Rolodogblog #6 #Montgomery

The smiley lady has a cheerful friend who is a cook and she has just moved across the Welsh border to a small town called Montgomery. We went up there not long after she had moved in. Our purpose was to help her settle in and explore. After a lovely lunch in her home we went walking over the fields and through a wood at the foot of the impressive ruins of Montgomery Castle.

I was off my lead and running freely and the smiley and cheerful friends were deep in chatter and ignoring me. I disappeared under some bushes and discovered a fantastic place to explore and hide. I didn't think they'd notice if I went off on my own for a while. Abandoned fox holes!

I could hear the ladies calling faintly as I went deeper and deeper underground, following an exciting trail of earthy scents. The cheerful lady's kind face suddenly appeared at one of the holes and I quickly ducked out of reach — I hadn't finished exploring yet.

'Don't worry too much; he'll come out when he's bored,' I heard the smiley lady say. I've done this a few times before you see.

At the furthest point from the voices (which were becoming more and more anxious) I discovered an exit. It was a vertical shaft but not to the open air. I had come out in an underground chamber of some sort with lots of different rooms leading off it. I went into one room and saw that the walls had ledges all the way around cut into the earth about half way up. The small doorway off the chamber led to another identical to this one and so it went on. What was this place?

A whole maze of rooms it seemed. I wondered whether I had stumbled across some long-hidden secret. Another passageway led upwards through a shaft and I wondered if that was into the castle itself.

I strained my listening ear and could hear the anxiety in the smiley lady's distant voice and decided it was time to reappear. I would make a mental note of where this labyrinth of rooms and the passageway to the castle lay.

I resurfaced and was immediately
scooped up by the smiley lady
who was smothering me in kisses,
brushing the dirt off my face and
telling me off all at the same time.
Mixed messages. Very confusing,
smiley lady.

She clipped the lead on to my
harness and we continued our walk
up the steep hill to the ruined
castle in silence. Not sure if the
smiley lady and cheerful cook were
out of breath with the exertion of
climbing or whether they had run
out of chit chat. Maybe they were
just cross with me.

#rololovestunnels
#onceajackrussell
#excitingdiscovery

Chapter 6

Rolo and Montgomery Castle

Once we reached the grounds of the ruined castle, the silence broke. The smiley lady loves ancient buildings, stones and trees as she thinks she can feel the life force and learn stories about the places by touching them. I've heard it all before. She started showing off her historical knowledge to the cheerful cook who was duly impressed, but I knew the smiley lady had read a guide book in advance and also committed to memory the facts on the information board.

'I bet you didn't know this: Montgomery was a strategic point in the power struggle between the Welsh and the English in the 13th century,' she started up.

'No, I had no idea. It doesn't look very important now,' said the cheery cook. Oh no, don't encourage her, I thought to myself, but she was off.

'You can see here, it's protected on three sides by

steep cliffs and valleys and the fourth side was level ground making a natural entrance which had to be heavily fortified.' The smiley lady waved her arms over the parapet and continued, 'Just a mile away was a vital ford crossing the River Camlad: a natural border between Wales and England.'

There's bound to be more, I thought, and sure enough...

'This was the traditional meeting point of the English and Welsh in an area known as the Marches. Welsh border security had always fallen to the Marcher lords, but then Prince Llewellyn began to rattle his sabre; he was just too powerful to deal with.'

'How do you know all this?' asked the cheery cook in amazement.

'She's reading it from the information board over your shoulder!' I wanted to shout. The smiley lady continued, a bit louder,

'Newly crowned Henry lll of England, 16-year-old son of King John, saw the sense in building a fortified castle on this rock during a visit to the area, encouraged by his senior advisor Hugh de Burgh. The old castle on the ford would be retained as a signalling post to warn of a Welsh advance.'

The smiley lady paused in her narration and the cheerful cook nodded with enthusiasm, or was she just being polite. A young man walking past overheard this history lesson and he too was impressed and joined the conversation.

'Don't encourage her or she will go on and on,' I thought.

'Bet you don't know we're standing on top of a maze of secret chambers!' I wished I could voice this discovery. Far more exciting.

I scampered about the ruins on my retractable lead trying to find the place where the secret passage came out. I found a grille over what appeared to be

a well beside the ruined tower and wondered if that
was the spot.

'Come on, Rolo, let's go home for tea,' said the smiley
lady pulling me away from my investigations.

When we were back in Wiltshire after our Welsh
weekend I couldn't wait to ask Athelstan about
Montgomery Castle and ask why it fell to ruin. I
also wanted to know whether he knew about the
existence of the underground rooms.

'Well, Montgomery was a very important castle for
a time, Little Pup, its purpose being to keep Prince
Llewellyn and his Welsh army out of England. The

The Secret Adventures of Rolo

original structure was built of wood from the inner keep outwards, but this was later replaced by stone,'

'Here we go, another history lesson,' I thought and settled down and dozed on and off as the tree dragon rambled.

'... begun in 1223 and Montgomery town was granted a royal charter in 1227 allowing the townspeople to hold markets and fairs, making it the oldest borough in Wales. The castle was huge and a military garrison grew up within its walls. The town sprang up at the foot of the rock to supply the fortress above.' The tree dragon paused.

I was always amazed by his ability to remember dates and come out with facts upon request.

'Montgomery was a typical medieval town built on a grid system.'

'...and little has changed today,' I interrupted, thinking we wouldn't get to the end before daybreak.

'But what happened to the castle?' I prompted, picturing the ruin I had visited at the weekend.

'Well, the castle's military importance lessened over time once peace was established between England and Wales other than those pesky dragons continuing the fight,' Athelstan mused,

'After the Battle of Montgomery during the English Civil War in 1644 the Parliamentarians defeated the Royalists and ordered the castle to be demolished. The town continued to grow in the shadow of the ruin on the rock. Montgomery became the county town of Montgomeryshire, a name the locals still use even though it has recently become part of Powys.'

'I found some underground rooms and a passageway through the rock up into the castle walls. Could they have been used for anything useful back then? Relieving a siege, perhaps?' I asked eagerly.

'Not that you need to know just now, Little Pup, but bear it in mind.' Athelstan faded back into the tree bark and left me standing in the middle of the forest staring at the tree trunk.

'Off you go then, Paddy Paws, no adventures tonight. An early night,' smiled Yulia, extinguishing her lantern.

Rolodogblog #7 #guineapigs

As you may remember, the smiley lady's father lives in a big house with some other people who are also aged 90 or thereabouts. We go and see Grandad Polo every week. I play blinking games with him and also protect him from anyone who comes in whether they are bringing lunch or a cup of tea and biscuits. I'm very good at security. Everybody in the big house, carers and residents, they all know and love me. I get lots of treats when the smiley lady isn't looking.

Today we went to see Grandad Polo.
I led the way up to his room,
pulling the smiley lady along the
corridors and when we arrived we
were dismayed to find his room
empty.

'Never mind, he must be in the
lounge,' said the smiley lady,
putting down the tin of homemade
rock cakes, and we set off along the
corridor. I went into the lounge
first, eager to find Grandad, and
sure enough there he was, sitting
in a circle with about ten of his
friends, and each of them had a
GUINEA PIG on their laps!

I thought all my Christmases had
come at once and was so eager to
greet Grandad and meet his little
furry friend, but I found myself
hauled out from the room on a very

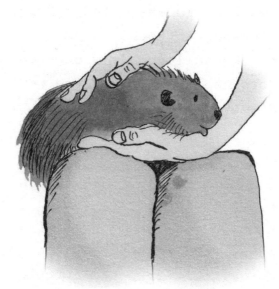

short lead before you could say
Jack Russell. I could hear Grandad
and his friends laughing as I was
marched out to sit in the car.

#notfair
#Ionlywantedtoplay
#rololovesguineapigs

Chapter 7

Rolo and the Jewel Collar

Another fascinating homework conversation overheard between my people at dinner time – this time about the Trojan Wars. The floppy haired boy wanted to know all about them.

The smiley lady wasn't much help. 'Beware of Greeks bearing gifts,' she said and then she mentioned a beautiful woman called Helen, a wooden horse and something about Achilles heel. Was that something you caught in public swimming pools, I wondered.

'Well, we're talking 3000BC,' said the floppy haired boy, chewing his pen thoughtfully.

'About the same time as the Bronze Age over here,' the smiley lady said, trying to be smart.

'And the Bedouins inhabiting the UAE,' I thought to myself.

I thought I'd have a word with Athelstan. He's bound

to know. Although I can't share my love of history with the floppy haired boy, I do enjoy finding out about the things he is interested in.

'Greek mythology is a fascinating topic, Little Pup,' said the tree dragon when I spoke to him later that night.

'You see the Trojan Wars are half true and half myth. The time tunnel can't take you to explore a myth, but I know another way. Fetch your jewel collar.'

I bounded straight home, excited that I was at last going to find out why Rhydian had returned the collar to me and what powers it might possibly have and where adventures might lead.

I stopped stock still when I opened the trapdoor because I could hear footsteps upstairs. I waited under the sink, holding my breath in case someone was going to come down to the kitchen for a glass of water.

The toilet flushed and the footsteps retreated. Phew! I dug under the cushion in my basket and found the jewel collar. I carried it in my teeth as before, back through the trapdoor and into the forest and set it at the foot of the Athelstan tree.

'Now, Little Pup, you have to put the jewel collar around your neck and fasten it,' the wise dragon said. I picked it up again.

I wondered how I was going to do that, and then I saw Yulia waving at me.

'Bring the collar over here!' she instructed.

The tiny woodland girl took the collar from me and I lay down flat so she could reach me as she clambered upon a tree root. Da was on hand to help too. Between them they managed to fasten it with the clear diamond type jewel at the base of my throat. I felt a tingling sensation and an intense heat around my neck and then something rather peculiar happened. My fur started to prickle. It felt like I was

137

wearing a suit of armour. I had the urge to run.

One minute I'm bounding through the long grass, the spiky new growth tickling my tummy, then my strides are getting longer – and l o n g e r – quite an achievement for short legs I can tell you! All of a sudden I can't feel the ground beneath my paws anymore – it's as if I am treading water in the air!

The Secret Adventures of Rolo

Wowee! I'm flying! My front paws are moving of
their own accord now, not diagonally opposite
with back paws like Spotty Dog (ask mum or dad
who that is if you don't know; he's a legend) but
rhythmically beating time up and down as if they
were wings.

Hold the front page – they ARE wings! This is surely
a dream! I'm a rescue Jack Russell who time travels
and blogs. I've only ever been a passenger before
now, flying across the sky with Rhydian the Welsh
dragon, and here I am soaring through the air under
my own steam!

From the corner of my eye I just catch the jewel
collar around my neck glowing.

Now what did the dragons do to travel so far back in
time? Think, Rolo, think.

'Well, you're really getting the hang of this!' a little
voice tinkled in my ear and I nearly fell from the sky.
Yulia must have jumped on my back when she

fastened the collar and I didn't even notice!

'Keep flapping your wings, Paddy Paws! You didn't think Athelstan would send you off on your first dragon experience on your own, did you? That's why Rhydian took the jewel collar from you in the first place, so you couldn't be like Gwyn and go off adventuring before you were ready.'

I wobbled a bit as I tried to turn to look at her. 'Can I have a dragon name for when I am being a dragon?' I asked.

'Good idea, what do you want to be called? You realise you can only be a dragon when you wear the jewel collar, don't you?'

Yes, I had already figured that out. Imagine if I had turned into a dragon for ever. What a shock that would be for the smiley lady, although no doubt the floppy haired boy would find it pretty cool!

'Rodor,' I said at once, 'that's what Alfred the Great

140

called me and I like it. He said it meant 'of the sky' and when I'm a dragon, that's pretty accurate.'

'That makes sense,' said Yulia.

'Now concentrate, Paddy Paws, I mean Rodor – you have to fly straight up through the clouds and then make a swooping figure of eight and remember to tilt your wings as you come back beneath the cloud level or we won't have travelled back in time at all,' she warned.

'Hold tight,' I shouted back to her but my voice was lost in the whooshing.

I needn't have worried – Yulia was clinging on for dear life! I was a bit of a novice at flying and completely in awe of the power of my new wings.

141

Chapter 8

Rolo and the Trojan Horse

We landed unobserved in a Middle Eastern town. I thought for a minute we were back in Dubai!

'Oh, Rodor, you forgot to tilt your wings. We are in modern day Western Turkey! Hisarlik, site of ancient Troy, yes, but about 5,000 years too late!' Yulia wailed.

Well, the Turks seemed too busy with their everyday lives to be noticing a girl sitting astride a small dragon wearing a jewelled collar, so we managed to sneak out of the town to a bit of wasteland and take off quickly, back up in the air. This time I completed the manoeuvre properly and remembered to tilt my wings at the appropriate moment just as we broke back through the cloud layer on our descent. We had arrived at the same spot but the scene that greeted us this time was very different. We were on the outside of a very high wall indeed.

'Yes, this looks about right,' said Yulia, as she jumped

down. 'Well done, Rodor. Welcome to Troy! We'd better get this collar off you so that you can be a dog again. You might blend in a little better as a dog than a dragon, don't you think?'

Yulia looked around for something to stand on so she could reach the buckle on the back of my neck. 'I'd better look after the collar for you,' she said, climbing onto a low wall.

As soon as Yulia unfastened the collar and removed it from my skin, I felt the same tingling sensation and glanced down at my paws and saw they were furry once more.

'Did I change colour as a dragon?' I asked her, licking my paws.

'You were a dragon not a chameleon,' she laughed and then added, 'no you still looked like Paddy Paws but with scales and wings and a funny tail.'

We sat down in the shade of an olive tree and I

don't think we looked out of place. There were dogs, children, men and women going about their business on the outside of the wall. It seemed this was a farming community.

'Athelstan told me to give you a bit of background about the Trojan War as we have arrived towards the end of it,' said Yulia as she tickled my ears.

I settled down to listen. The hot sun was making me sleepy.

'Well, it all started with Helen. No, let's rewind a bit; legend has it that it started with a game between the Greek gods.'

I put my head on her lap and listened.

'There was a wedding between Greek King Peleus and Thetis, a goddess of the sea. To witness their marriage all the gods had been invited except Eris, goddess of discord. In a rage, and rather like the bad fairy in a well-known story, Eris threw a golden apple labelled 'To the fairest' among the goddesses hoping to cause mischief. Hera, Athene and Aphrodite each laid claim to the apple which came from the tree of the Hesperides and each wanted the prize.

'Zeus, chief of all the Greek gods, decided it wasn't in his best interest to mediate this competition for fear of upsetting the goddesses and instead he bade Hermes, the winged messenger, to take the contestants from Mount Olympus to the mortal Trojan prince, Paris, son of King Priam, so he could choose which of the three deserved the prize.

'Each goddess appeared in a dream to Paris and tried to bribe him to choose her as the winner of the golden apple: Hera offered him the wealth to rule over Europe and Asia; Athene offered him heroism and victory. Troy eventually chose Aphrodite, because she promised him love in the form of the most beautiful woman in the world – Helen.

'Helen had been pursued by all the Greek kings

because of her legendary beauty. Problem was Helen was already married to Menelaus, king of Sparta. Paris claimed his prize by running away with Helen; he sailed back to Troy with her, and hid behind a big wall in his father's kingdom, besieged within the city for ten years despite many attacks by the Greeks who sailed in a thousand ships to reclaim their lost queen. Lots of heroes with names beginning with the letter 'A' were involved: Agamemnon, Achilles, Aeneas and Ajax. They mostly perished. Now it's reached a kind of stalemate and that's where you come in,' Yulia finished her explanation. I was almost asleep.

'Come on, Paddy Paws, you are to meet Odysseus, King of Ithaca, to see if you can resolve the problem by ending the siege of Troy.' She shoved my head off her lap and stood up.

'I thought I was Rodor now,' I said sleepily.

'That's going to be your dragon name. You're back to Paddy Paws when you are being you,' she countered.

'Aren't you coming with me?' I asked, feeling a bit anxious about the task.

'This is your adventure not mine – don't worry though I'll be close at hand. There's something I want to do whilst we're here.'

In this time of war, everyone was suspicious of strangers but nobody took much notice of me because I was just a dog.

I sauntered up to the guards on the big wooden doors of the palace and did my best meerkat impression – up on my back legs. This charm offensive usually works and it didn't let me down this time.

'Hey, look at this, kyon,' said one of the Greek guards.

I accepted a piece of bread and went within the walls unchallenged.

King Odysseus was easy to find. He was having a war planning meeting and his army leaders were fed up after nine long years of fighting, with no visible means of removing the Trojans or of rescuing Helen and returning her to her Greek husband so they could all pack up and go home.

I was pleased to find I could converse with him and jumped up on his lap from where I could inspect him more closely. Odysseus was a great big dark-skinned man with thick curly hair, a large nose and a black beard. He smelled of olives. I licked him under his chin and his troubled face broke into a wide smile. He stroked me absent-mindedly whilst he addressed his war council.

'We have tried everything to break into the fortress. There is no way in. What else can we do?'

'Trickery,' I whispered in his ear. 'You can trick your way in.'

If the king was surprised that a small dog could

address him, he didn't show it.

'And just what do you propose, kyon?'

I had the full attention of the war council now and stepped on to the table importantly. I was winging it a bit because I didn't really have an idea as such; I was just remembering stuff I'd overheard in conversation between the floppy haired boy and the smiley lady.

'The way I see it is you need to strike camp and leave the area: disperse the army,' I said boldly.

There were mutterings from the army leaders.

'What trickery is this?' said one, equally dark and hairy.

'You don't really leave. It's an illusion you are creating. Let the Trojans think you have abandoned your siege. Simply go away and hide.'

'How does that get us into Troy?' said a third dark and hairy man.

'Erm, here's the rest of the plan: you need to leave them a gift, right outside the gates, one they can't resist. They will open the gates to take the gift inside and then you can surprise them in attack.'

The muttering in the room rose to a crescendo.

'What kind of gift?' someone shouted.

'You!' said a new voice. 'Yes, that's it! We leave the cute kyon outside the gate and they will want to keep him so when they open the gates we all rush in!'

This stupid suggestion was met with guffaws of laughter around the room and then unbelievably they started nodding their heads in approval. Were they really this dim? No, this plan was never going to work! I had to somehow get them to think about making a big statue on wheels. Something that soldiers could hide in.

I held up my paw for silence and commanded their attention again. I explained the second part of my plan.

'But we can't fit the whole army inside a wooden animal!' said the one who had wanted to leave me at the gate.

'Build it big enough to hide thirty of your best soldiers.' I was warming to my theme. 'The rest of the army will be waiting for a signal not too far away, and once the gift is inside the walls of Troy, in the dead of night, the soldiers can sneak out and open the gates from the inside to let the rest of the hidden army in, snatch Helen, sail home. There we are. Problem solved. Job done.'

My idea was met with stunned silence. They all looked at each other. You could have heard a pin drop.

One of the men started drawing up a plan for a wooden animal. Its features looked remarkably like mine!

'I'm not sure that they will know what that is. No disrespect young kyon,' said the King. 'We need to make something more recognisable.'

'A lion!' suggested one.

'Too hard to draw,' said the planner.

'A serpent!'

'Not very appealing,' said King Odysseus. 'I don't think they'd open the gates for that!'

'What about a horse?' said one of the men who hadn't spoken previously.

At last, we're getting there!

'Excellent idea! All men desire a fine horse. They are bound to fall for it,' I encouraged.

The war council planned through the night and made drawings of a fine model horse, big enough to hide some soldiers inside.

I stayed to watch, and other men with knowledge of woodworking were dragged from their beds to begin building the gift. There was no time to lose.

The following day the Greek army took down their tents and made a great show of leaving the area for the first time in ten years. I had no doubt that the Trojans were watching their enemy from within the walls of Troy. I hoped this plan would work. The army went and hid a short distance away on the other side of a vast olive grove and waited patiently until nightfall.

The large wooden horse was wheeled to the gate under the cover of darkness. I sat underneath the horse on the wheel box.

It didn't take long for the Trojans to be curious enough to open the gate a crack and send someone out to have a look. I held my breath and crouched down.

A voice shouted from within the walls,

'What is it, Spyros?'

'A Greek offering… looks like a horse.' So far so good.

'We had better burn it!' I held my breath.

A big bearded face leaned down to inspect the horse and saw me. Oh no, this was never going to work. I hardly dared breathe.

'It has fine carving detail on it and I think Paris will like it for Helen. There's a little kyon with it. It's too good to destroy. Let's bring it inside so we can have a closer look.'

'Don't look a gift horse in the mouth,' I thought, then remembered that was the wrong saying. 'Beware of Greeks bearing gifts,' I corrected myself, but I didn't voice it out loud of course. It seemed the plan was working. I let out a long sigh. This was close!

The huge gates creaked open just enough and several Trojan soldiers came out to wheel the wooden horse inside. I managed to jump off inside the gate and hide behind a column.

'Where's that little dog gone? Helen would like him and I'd like to be the one to gift him to her,' said the bearded one.

'No dog here, you must be imagining things,' said one of the watchmen.

Just then a horn blew, signalling the end of the soldiers' night watch. They parked the horse inside the gates, secured them shut and turned in for the night. The Trojans must have felt pretty secure inside their fortress after such a long siege, because they didn't send out another guard to replace those who had turned in for the remainder of the night.

Everything seemed to be going well and I stared at the horse, expecting the trapdoor in the belly to spring open as soon as the soldiers had disappeared. That was the plan.

I heard a bit of a commotion inside the horse and moved closer.

'The bolt's stuck. Kyon are you there? Design fault. Quickly! Can you let us out?'

Without further ado I jumped up on the wooden

base and worked the latch from the outside with my teeth.

The trapdoor flew open and Greek soldiers tumbled out in a pile of arms and legs, untangled themselves quietly and sprang up drawing their swords. I left them to it as they were trying to move noiselessly with lots of shushing as they set about opening the big gate from the inside. I wanted a look at Helen whilst I was here.

I ran through the city of Troy and quickly found my way to the palace. Again, I didn't have much trouble sneaking past the royal guards and finding the sleeping quarters. No one bothered to stop a cute dog in the middle of the night. Then I halted in my tracks because in front of me, lounging on a silk cushion was the most beautiful woman I had ever seen. She had long fair hair and big blue eyes; I felt sure men could drown in their sea of blue.
As I drew nearer with my own eyes out on stalks, Helen saw me and bent down to lift me onto her lap. She had something in her hand and it dug me in the

ribs as she picked me up – the jewel collar!

How on earth did she get that?! My first thought was that I had to get it back or I would be stuck in Ancient Greece for ever!

As she engulfed me in a wave of perfume and hugged me to her chest I caught sight of Yulia, hiding behind a coffer, miming wildly and pointing frantically at the collar.

I submitted to kisses and cuddles from the beautiful lady and wondered how I was going to retrieve the collar, when suddenly fair Helen had the idea to put the jewel collar around my neck.

'It looks just your size!' she murmured as she fastened it.

I felt myself tingling all over and knew at once what was happening – I was turning back into a dragon! I had to get out of here quickly.

'By Zeus what creature are you? Surely you've come from Hades!' she squealed in fright and dropped me on the floor. Yulia seized the moment and took a running jump from the coffer and leapt onto my back.

'Go, Rodor!' Yulia shouted and I advanced towards an open window; I didn't need any encouragement. I stretched my wings and flew as high as I could, across the city and barely noticed all the Greek soldiers spilling in through the gates as I soared over the walls of Troy and up and up into the clouds. I felt sick from the suddenness of the ascent but there was no time to be fainthearted! We had to get back to the present day and home before dawn!

Whoa! Better concentrate…steady Rodor…both front paws level and away we go again, beating in time, one two, one two…

I stopped flapping my paws and came to a rather ungainly landing in the forest at Athelstan's feet – or where they would be if he had any visible. The tree dragon appeared before me and seemed to be smiling. His woody eyes twinkled as he greeted me,

'Well, well, little pup, are my ancient eyes deceiving me or are you looking a little dragony?'

Yulia jumped down and then bade me come over to the tree root so she could unfasten the jewel collar. My fur tingled and yes it was fur again and my wings had turned back into paws and my tail had gone from long and pointy to an upright flag. I was Rolo once more.

I was really worried about the time we had been missing on our Ancient Greek adventure because I thought the smiley lady would be distraught if she opened the kitchen door in the morning to find an empty basket.

'You didn't tell him, did you Yulia?' said Athelstan gravely.

'Didn't tell me what?' I couldn't keep the panic from

my voice.

'When you are wearing the jewel collar, you are going to a different dimension of myths and legends. It's as if real time stands still, so no one will have missed you as they won't know you have gone,' the woodland girl said matter-of-factly.

Oh well, at least I know that now. I would have liked to have stayed to see what happened to Helen and whether the Greek plan to conquer the Trojans worked. I'm sure the boy with floppy hair will tell me sooner or later.

After Athelstan faded into the tree and Yulia was picking her way over the roots to her underground home, I asked her out of curiosity how Helen had got her hands on the collar.

Yulia ignored my question, but did say that she would keep the jewel collar safe and ready for our next adventure.

The Secret Adventures of Rolo

Rolodogblog #8 #afishytale

Walking along the bank of the River Kennet the smiley lady is singing away to herself and admiring the bird life. She spots a pair of tree creepers and a couple of nuthatches and is very excited.

It's only January, but it's been a mild winter and the birds seem to be nesting already. A cheery robin chirrups us on our way, then we stop suddenly and the smiley lady puts a restraining hand on my harness. We have just disturbed a great grey heron doing a spot of angling and helping himself to a trout.

I barked and this was enough to disturb him. He took off vertically, a great swooping of wings and

in his haste dropped his snack.
The poor fish lay flapping on the
bank, twitching head and tail,
desperately trying to get back
in the river. Quick as a flash I
wriggled free from the smiley
lady's grasp; her face turned to
horror as she thought I was going
to eat the fish.

'No, Rolo!' she shouted.

I picked up the poor floppity thing
in my mouth as gently as I could
without using my teeth and dropped
it over the side of the bank into
the river from whence it had
come. It made a splosh and then
lay motionless on the surface for
a moment. Just when I thought I
had been too late with my rescue,
there was a flicker of life; the fish
gave a little shimmy and wiggled

downwards to hide and recover amongst the weed in the depths of the Kennet.

'Good boy,' the smiley lady said, when she realised what I had done. She reached in her pocket and pulled out a doggy biscuit as a reward.

#rolosavestheday

Chapter 9

Rolo and the Cardiff Dragon

I was in my cage on the back seat of the car and the smiley lady was making very slow progress along the inside lane of the westbound carriageway of the M4 motorway, the busy highway which connects England and Wales by means of a road bridge. The smiley lady saw the toll sign indicating that payment would be required to cross into Wales and asked the floppy haired boy to find coins in her purse.

'So we have to pay to go into Wales but not to come out? Where's the logic in that?' he said.

Taking in the magnificent view of the Severn Estuary from the impressive bridge, the floppy haired boy noticed that the needle on the fuel gauge on the dashboard was now well past the red zone and hovering dangerously on 'E' for empty. He tentatively broached the subject with his mum.

'Oh, no! We need to find a petrol station quick –

we're pretty much running on fresh air,' the smiley lady exclaimed, gripping the steering wheel rather more tightly than usual, her shoulders went up round her ears.

The tense motorist had no idea that 'Gwasanaeth' meant 'service station' in Welsh. By the time the floppy haired boy had tried to pronounce the name out loud the smiley lady had already driven past two. She was not so smiley now – I could see her reflection in the rear-view mirror. She was desperate to reach the next service station without running out of fuel.

At last the long Welsh 'G' word loomed into sight again and I could hear the clicking of the indicator as the smiley lady almost free-wheeled the empty car onto the slip road, much to the annoyance of the motorists stuck behind her. She willed the car up to the fuel pumps and I held my breath... we'd made it!

The smiley lady pulled up the handbrake, pulled a lever in the door to release the fuel cap and turned

'*Jewel Dog and the Dragons*'

off the engine. At the pump, she started fussing with the nozzle; clicking the trigger in an attempt to get the indicator back to zero before starting to fill up the tank. I saw the floppy haired boy slide down in the passenger seat, probably bored with this very long journey. I knew how he felt, but didn't think it would help if I started barking like I usually do at petrol stations.

Filling the empty tank seemed to take an eternity, but at last the pump made a resounding click to indicate that the tank was full and I watched the smiley lady carefully replace the nozzle in its cradle. And then the smiley lady could be heard muttering very loudly indeed and slapping the side of the car with her hand. Very uncharacteristic! Other customers paused in the middle of refuelling their vehicles and peered over to see what was going on with the crazy lady at pump number 2.

'What's up Mum?' the floppy haired boy let down his window.

167
The Secret Adventures of Rolo

'I've gone and put the wrong fuel in! I can't believe it! All the fuel pipes at this pump are black; petrol is usually green and diesel is black. My car is diesel and I've filled it with petrol – this is a disaster!'

The smiley lady had enough sense not to start the engine and instead released the handbrake and got the floppy haired boy and a sympathetic lorry driver to help push the car away from the pumps and park it safely at the side of the garage forecourt so they could ring the emergency services to see what was to be done. Putting the wrong type of fuel in your vehicle is a very expensive mistake it seems and also very time consuming as the tank would have to be drained and cleaned by a fuel disposal technician before the correct fuel could be added.

The floppy haired boy got out of the passenger seat and came round to my door to let me out to stretch my legs. I think he was trying to get his bearings so as to be of some help when giving a location to the rescue people.

I saw that the garage was directly opposite a large and very imposing hotel set back high on the hillside above the motorway. Looking across the carriageway, I caught sight of an enormous flagpole at the hotel entrance, sporting a very large Welsh flag, easily identifiable by its proud red dragon emblazoned on a green and white background, flapping and snapping on its taut mooring in the stiff breeze. The floppy haired boy had seen it too.

'That should help with the location,' I thought to myself.

I could hardly believe what happened next, and rubbed my eyes vigorously with my paws to make sure I was awake and not dreaming.

From the garage forecourt I spied a large red dragon in a very great hurry, flying at and seemingly trying to hide in, the furiously furling flag. I glanced at the floppy haired boy but he was looking in the opposite direction.

The dragon appeared to be in a bit of a state about something and was quite literally spitting fire.

Suddenly a spark from the dragon's mouth scorched the giant flag; I hardly dared watch as the ember flashed and grew, the glowing red fire spreading quickly across the flammable material, literally gobbling it up. Within seconds, all that was left was the flagpole and a flurry of ash swirling in the air, and the big waving dragon flag was no more. No one on the forecourt seemed to notice, certainly not the floppy haired boy. The dragon had completely disappeared.

Meanwhile the floppy haired boy had suggested to the smiley lady giving the big flag outside the hotel as a landmark and we all got back inside the car. I heard her say into her mobile phone,

'We are opposite a big hotel with a very large Welsh flag,' to the patient roadside assistance operator. The smiley lady tailed off as she did a double take,

The Secret Adventures of Rolo

'Well, I must be seeing things,' she said.

'I could have sworn there was an enormous flag flying there just a few seconds ago...someone must have whipped it down pretty quick! Okay, then opposite a great big empty flagpole.' Luckily the rescue company knew exactly where she meant.

Twenty minutes later a Fuel Special Handling Technician arrived on the forecourt in his big yellow van, lights a-flashing. The first thing he did was put up a folding warning sign behind the car forbidding naked flames, mobile phones, cigarettes or anything else in the vicinity which might give off a spark during this very dangerous fuel draining procedure. I supressed a smile; it was just as well that fiery dragon had disappeared!

Forty minutes later our rescuer disconnected the last wire from his highly technical van. With all its tanks and pipes in the back, I thought it looked as though it might be possible to time travel in it like I had seen with the floppy haired boy in the 'Back to the

Future' films.

'All done, madam. Next time best read the labels on the pumps,' he said rather smugly as he wiped his hands on a cloth and took payment from the not so smiley lady. He packed up his signs, slammed the door shut and waved us on our way. All in a day's work.

I could hardly wait for nightfall to report to Athelstan,

'So there's this red dragon flying about near Cardiff and he seems to be setting fire to Welsh flags!' Athelstan stroked his imaginary beard wisely and said,

'Some dragons think they can hide in dragon-shaped objects; it was a power that we used to have. You'd best go investigate.'

The tree dragon used his own powers to summon Rhydian. Before you could say Jack Russell the two of us were airborne and heading off in a westerly direction.

Once more we were following the M4 motorway towards Cardiff, but from the air this time – definitely quicker by dragon and we didn't have to pay the toll! We had a marvellous view of the Severn Bridge and I could even recognise the service station where we had experienced the fuelling mishap opposite the big hotel's still empty flagpole.

On into the city we flew. Cardiff was easily located from above, identifiable by its docks and new Waterfront development. The Principality Stadium stood proudly above the old city like a giant spun sugar basket. There was a golden clock on an ornate tall tower, and seeing the time I realised how quickly we had travelled by dragon.

Rhydian seemed to know exactly where he was going and homed in on the grey concave roof of Cardiff City Hall, upon which we immediately saw a very impressive statue of a yawning dragon with its mouth wide open. The dragon was mounted on a pedestal which topped the dome. I thought for the second time that day that I must be seeing things. I could have sworn I saw a spark fly out from the dragon statue's mouth. I said as much to Rhydian.

'Look, there's another one,' and sure enough another red ember shot out into the air.

Rhydian used all his skill and agility to land on the domed roof, muttering under his breath as he tripped over the ornate plaster shell and garland decorations which greatly hindered his landing. Then he called out to the sparking dragon.

A confident red dragon, with the same kind of look about him as Rhydian but a bit smaller in stature, came out from his hiding place behind the dragon statue. For a moment he stood glaring at us. We must have been a strange sight – a small dog riding a dragon – and he was probably wondering what on earth we were doing on his roof.

He looked familiar to me and I waited patiently for him to speak. The dragon towered above us and then suddenly sprang cat-like onto the head of the yawning dragon statue. He exchanged formal greetings with Rhydian in their own peculiar language as was the dragon custom and once this was done the tension between the two dragons seemed to ease.

Quite unexpectedly the red dragon switched to heavily accented English and, drawing himself up to full height, spoke in a sing song voice,

'Bore da! I am Reod, guardian of the noble city of Cardiff; you can see me on all the rubbish bins.' I suppressed a snigger behind my paw.

'You again!' said Rhydian. Of course, they had met before. No wonder that I recognised him – this was one of the skirmishing dragons!

The flamboyant dragon paused to preen himself thinking we were impressed. If Reod was disappointed by lack of audience reaction he didn't show it. I heard Rhydian whisper under his breath 'young whippersnapper!'

A true performer, Reod took a deep breath and then exhaled slowly through his nostrils as if he were completing breathing exercises in a yoga class. He stood back expectantly, building anticipation.

Then Reod did a curious thing: he lurched forward, going down on all fours, leaving his back legs on the pedestal, and peered over the side of the dome, gripping the ledge with his front claws and lowering his face towards the ground as if looking for something. Tossing his head from left to right, he said to no one in particular,

'What, no fans today?'

I glanced at Rhydian but he hadn't a clue what this Welsh dragon was doing. The young dragon reeled his body back in like a slinky spring and manoeuvred himself back on top of his perch once more.

Rhydian told him I had come for a history lesson.
I tried to make myself more comfortable on the
domed roof. I sat on the ledge provided by the
architectural decorations and did 'clown eyes' as
I anticipated the lengthy telling of Welsh history.
Reod intoned some strange words adding to the
theatrical effect, then he switched back to English
and started to describe opposing armies meeting in
battle, and the significance of their two colours, red
against white.

'The Welsh marched into battle under the banner
of the red dragon and the West Saxons, or English,
rallied under a white dragon flag,' he began.

Just as Reod was about to continue the narrative I
heard children's' voices shouting up from the ground
and the red dragon jumped down, getting into the
same position as before, with his big red face peering
down towards the ground.

'There it is, look, up there, there it goes again, look!' Excited voices filled the air and little people were waving and pointing up to the grey dragon statue on the dome.

I was alarmed for a minute: were Rhydian and Reod visible from the ground? The children would surely be terrified if they could see dragons!

The Secret Adventures of Rolo

Then I worked out just what the children could see: little sparks coming from the mouth of the dragon statue every time Reod spoke, and the more animated he got, the more frequently the embers flew. From the ground I bet they appeared to be coming right out from the Civic Hall dragon statue's mouth!

'Ah, there they are, my little fan club. Right on time. I do this to entertain them as they go in and out of school – bless them they love it!' And Reod puffed out another red ember which landed harmlessly on the roof but this time a bit too near my paw for comfort. Rhydian stamped on the spark to extinguish it.

'Steady on,' he hissed angrily.

The young red dragon ignored Rhydian and smiled at a Welsh flag being waved up at him by one of his adoring fans. I was scared he might set fire to it. The children below had lost interest and moved on; the spark show from the stone dragon on the dome was over for today it seemed.

Rhydian glared at Reod saying, 'You should be more careful – humans aren't supposed to see us. What's all this about, anyway, you trying to hide in a Welsh flag?'

'Oh, that little mishap – I was testing the art of hiding in dragon shaped things like my ancestors could, don't tell me you've never done that.' The young dragon furrowed his brow and seemed deep in concentration.

'Now then, where was I?' he settled down to storytelling once more.

'I need to explain something first: the name Wales came from the Saxon 'Wiales' which meant 'strangers'.'

'Nothing strange about the Welsh, I can assure you!' snapped Rhydian.

'Who is telling this story?' retorted Reod.
The red dragon narrated with the ease of one
accustomed to the stage,

'The Battle of Tintern in the 6th century was one
of many clashes during long years' of conflict and
border disputes between the Saxons and the Welsh.
Men fought hand to hand and toe to toe locked
in long and bloody battle, whilst the red dragon
and the white dragon representing the armies also
engaged in deadly aerial combat, inflicting terrible
pain and damage on each other. It was deadlock in
the air and neither could gain the upper claw with
his opponent, which was reflected in the continuing
struggle between the armies on the ground.'

Listening to the tale, I could almost smell the mud
and blood stench of the fierce battle. The narrating
dragon was dancing about around the dome waving
his claws and twisting this way and that, as if he was
enacting the battle from both sides. Then continuing
his narrative,

'Long hours passed. Dark clouds were threatening to swallow up the battlefield as creeping night covered the conflict like a blanket…'

I was drifting off to sleep on my rooftop perch, lulled by the lilting accent of the Welsh dragon as he recounted every detail of the battle.

Suddenly Reod gave an alarming screech. Rhydian shot up in the air. I jumped up and just managed to stop myself sliding off the roof!

Reod acted all parts of the next scene, throwing himself around with gusto as he narrated, 'As if from nowhere an unfamiliar dragon burst through the darkening sky to join the conflict, sending a scorching flame of fiery breath in the direction of the red dragon, seemingly choosing to side with the white dragon.

'Faced by two opponents, the fierce and proud red dragon suddenly found himself unfairly outnumbered, two against one, and there was nothing he could do. His instincts told him to stay and fight, or die.

'He fought on bravely and hopelessly against both attackers until, terribly wounded and with a heavy heart, the red dragon conceded defeat and slunk away to nurse his wounds whilst the white dragon postured triumphantly and celebrated what was, in truth, an unfair victory.'

Reod explained, 'The white dragon made a terrible error in dragonlore by not acknowledging in any way the help of the mysterious dragon. Instead, he boasted of his own fighting prowess. The white dragon stood proud and victorious and shook his claw at the slumped and bloodied back of the retreating red dragon.

'The snubbed dragon stranger, however, was very angry. As the three dragons departed the scene, each in different directions, the human armies on the battleground below remained locked in combat, neither side giving an inch and oblivious of the dragon fight overhead. Full of vengeance at not having his role in the victory acknowledged, the dragon stranger spat his wrath at the ground. This sparked a bolt of lightning, which by misfortune struck the Welsh leader Tewdrig, who astride his horse was giving battle orders to his men.

Reod continued, 'Tewdrig fell to the ground instantly, his chainmail smouldering. The Welsh army could not believe what they had just seen: their leader struck by lightning. Was it a sign, they wondered?

'The Welsh heir Meurig picked up the battle cry and rallied the men. The Saxons roared and charged, seizing the advantage of confusion, but the Welsh roared back, defiant and determined. Little ground was gained on that battlefield and both armies went home angry and depleted in number as there were many casualties on both sides.

'The Welsh claimed a marginal victory that day, but Tewdrig's death three days later caused by the freak lightning strike made it a hollow victory.

'The dragon stranger would not forget the breach of manners shown by the white dragon. He scorched and destroyed every white battle standard on the field to ensure the white dragon's image would not be seen again and the dragon himself disappeared from the skies, harbouring his grudge.

'And that is precisely why you haven't seen a white dragon flag leading the English into battle from that day to this…' Reod folded his wings and bowed his head to indicate his story was done. 'And why the red and white dragons still combat in the air whenever they meet.'

Of course the dragon was telling his own story, about him and Alba, and underneath his bluster he was still smarting at the wrongfulness of unfair defeat despite the great number of years which had passed since the Battle of Tintern.

The feeling of anger still glowed within the Welsh dragon like a red ember. It was raw and ready to ignite and the dragon seemed able to puff out little flames at will, as if releasing the valve on a pressure cooker, probably as a result of this smouldering injustice.

I wondered if the puffing was a spark malfunction and Reod simply couldn't control it.

'Let's go,' Rhydian said suddenly, 'and you, be more careful with your flame throwing antics,' he warned as we took our leave of Reod, leaving him where we had found him, hiding behind the stone dragon on the Civic Hall dome. We took to the air with me clinging round Rhydian's neck again.

'Such an upstart!' said Rhydian. 'I am the true Welsh dragon!' I didn't know what to say to that.

I slept most of the journey home, but something was bothering me.

'Why didn't I need the jewel collar to go and see that dragon?' I leaned forward to ask Rhydian as we came down to land in the forest.

'Because we are dealing in real time and not myth or legend,' he replied quite simply, as I jumped onto the forest floor.

'So dragons are real then, not fantasy?' but he didn't answer and suddenly disappeared. Athelstan chose not to reveal himself – he must be having an early night. Nothing else for it but to go home and sleep in my basket. Boy was I tired and yes I dreamed of dragons.

Chapter 10

Rolo in the Underworld

Whilst the smiley lady and the floppy haired boy were out one day, I climbed up on the chair so I could take a look at the book of Greek mythology which had been left open on the table.

Pawing through the pages, I came across a chapter about Hades. I found it really interesting and thought I would have a word with Athelstan to see if this was another Greek adventure I might be able to go on.

When the house fell silent I rushed out to find the tree dragon.

'What is it this time, Little Pup?' asked Athelstan.

'What can you tell me about Hades?' I said, coming straight to the point.

'Hades the Greek god, you mean? Well…'

All ears, I settled down at the foot of the tree to listen. I saw from the corner of my eye that Yulia had also come out to listen to the story.

'Hades was the brother of Zeus and Poseidon. He was third in the pecking order – Zeus ruled the gods from Mount Olympus, Poseidon ruled the sea and Hades was given the Underworld, but he was also the god of wealth. His name means 'invisible', Athelstan continued.

'Mmmm, interesting,' I thought.

'The Underworld was a dark and dismal domain. Hades decided that anyone who entered his underground kingdom would never be permitted to leave. It was the ultimate resting place.' This was chilling.

'I suppose you want to go there?' he said, looking down at me.

To be honest the tree dragon wasn't really selling it

to me, but I am naturally curious and I could see the twinkling of the jewel collar in Yulia's hand, so I thought 'YOLO, why not?'

I lay down at the foot of the tree so Yulia could fasten the collar that would facilitate the journey to this mythological place and asked,

'Has anyone ever come back from Hades?'

'Why yes, Heracles, Orpheus and Odysseus all returned from the Underworld, if their stories are to be believed.'

Well, at least that was a small crumb of comfort!

'I think I'll pass on this adventure thanks, Paddy Paws, I mean Rodor,' said Yulia as she adjusted the collar and watched my fur turn to scales.

'You'll need this,' said Athelstan and he dropped a silver coin from the tree. It looked suspiciously like the one I'd brought back from Peter Long on a previous adventure in medieval England.

Yulia picked up the coin and tucked it under the jewel collar and told me not to lose it and she also warned me to be careful not to eat anything.

All down to me then, this adventure. Oh well, no point in hanging about. Let's get on with it. What was that saying? 'Curiosity killed the…' Yes, well, it wasn't going to kill a Jack Russell!

I took to the skies and ascended over the tree tops and rose vertically through the clouds, hoping I could get the figure of eight and the wing dipping bit right otherwise who knows where in myth or legend I might end up! It did occur to me that without Yulia to take the collar off I'd have to remain a dragon, but didn't think that would be too much of a problem.

I came down to land beside a river whose water was as black as oil. It was eerily quiet and I wondered if I was in the right place. There were no signs saying 'Underworld'. Mist swirled about adding to the creepy atmosphere of the scene. Was this the right place? I didn't have to wait long to find out.

I heard the whooshing of moving water and a boat glided into view and pulled up alongside the bank. A hooded figure motioned me to get in the boat. He didn't seem surprised to be taking a dragon passenger.

'I am Charon and I will take you across the River Acheron but only if you have money to pay me,' he said.

I remembered the silver coin tucked in my collar and moved closer to the strange boatman so he

The Secret Adventures of Rolo

could remove it. His fingers were all bone and I thought he might be a skeleton underneath that hooded robe.

'I'll have a return ticket please,' I said politely, remembering a ferry journey across the River Dart with the smiley lady where I had to have my own ticket.

'One-way fare only. There is no return,' said the cheerless Charon as he cast off from the bank and used a big stick to punt the craft across the river. I hoped he meant that there was no cheap day return ticket and wondered how I would purchase another single as I didn't have any coins left, but I couldn't be worrying about that just now. We bumped the bank on the other side and the scary ferryman tied up the boat and motioned for me to alight.

I turned round to ask what time the return ferry left but he had already disappeared in his ghostly craft. I fought hard against an impending sense of doom.

'Right, Rolo, I mean Rodor – best claw forward,'
I said out loud to nobody, but saying it gave me
courage.

A huge dark and foreboding palace loomed ahead of
me. There was nothing else for it; I knew I had to
go in.

Guarding the door was the most terrifying dog I had
ever seen in my life. It looked a bit like the Roman
dog Brutus I'd met in Pompeii, but this was much
scarier as it had three heads. The creature seemed
to be having an argument with itself. I edged a little
nearer, grateful for my dragon disguise, else I feared
I would be devoured. I tried to pull myself up to full
height hoping to intimidate the snapping creature.

'Another one for the circus,' snapped the dog head
nearest me.

'You'd better come in,' said another.

'This way then,' said the third. 'Hurry up! And shut

The Secret Adventures of Rolo

the door behind you.'

All three dog heads glared at me. They were slavering wildly as if they hadn't eaten for a week. I saw they were tethered to a post – three iron collars all forged together and one very heavy-duty link chain keeping them there.

Well, this seemed to be going quite well – I hadn't met with any resistance and didn't give them a backward glance as I trotted on.

The massive wooden door creaked open and I tiptoed in. I tried to quell my terrier shake over which I had little control, even though I was temporarily a dragon. There was a horrible stench in the air – I couldn't identify the source of it, but it smelt a bit like a dustbin which desperately needed emptying.

To my surprise, amid all this gloom and decay, there sitting by an open fire was a beautiful young woman. She had long hair and wore flowing robes and sumptuous jewellery and the table next to her was groaning under the weight of freshly prepared food. But she clearly wasn't happy.

The poor lady was sobbing as if her heart would break. And, as I drew nearer, I could tell from her less than beautiful red and blotchy face that she had been crying for some time. I approached cautiously as I didn't want to scare her.

She must have heard me – I wasn't very light on my claws.

'Come here, sweet little drakon in a necklace!' She kerbed her sobs. 'What are you doing here in this miserable place? Has my husband sent you as a present to cheer me up? That's very kind of him – he is trying, although he doesn't have much of a clue.' Her voice was soft and friendly.

The lovely lady scooped me up in her arms and set me on her lap. Well, I couldn't look that scary after all. I forgot all about being a dragon and started licking away her tears. She smelt nice.

'Ooh, that tickles!' she squealed.

I found that I could speak to her and told her about the manner of my arrival.

'Oh, Cerberus wouldn't stop you coming in; he's only there to stop anyone leaving,' and with that she started crying again.

This was a bit awkward. When I am a cute Jack Russell I can usually cheer people up because I snuggle in and they cuddle me back and they feel a lot better. I'm small, soft and furry. Not too sure that this works when I'm a scaly dragon!

'What's a pretty girl like you doing in a place like this?' I used my best chat up line.

'My name is Persephone and I have been brought here against my will. Hades fell in love with me so he kidnapped me – opened up the earth and I fell through the crack. Right in front of my mother's eyes. That's how I came to be here in this horrible place. I would give anything to be able to leave. My mother Demeter is beside herself with worry. She is goddess of the harvest and has taken herself away from the earth to mourn my loss, which means there are no crops and everything on earth is barren. It's as if the world has come to an end. Hades will not give me up and my mother will not stop mourning. I just don't know what is going to happen. I seem to be causing a global disaster.'

'Ooh, that sounds familiar,' I thought, remembering Helen of Troy, and I tried to snuggle in to comfort her but it wasn't really working. Instead I sort of head-butted Persephone in the ribs. Dragons are not very cuddly it seems.

Suddenly there came the sound of approaching hoofbeats and the clattering of wheels and in front of my eyes a chariot pulled by four shiny black horses came to a screeching halt right inside that large gloomy hall. The draught they brought with them almost extinguished the fire.

'What have we here?' A voice boomed down like thunder as a huge man alighted from the chariot and I was hoisted into the air by yet another strong dark and hairy Greek arm and dangled in front of a bulbous nose for inspection.

'I didn't order a drakon!' Hades roared, 'they've sent the wrong pet for you!' he turned to Persephone and for a terrible moment I thought he was going to fling me into the fire!

'But he's cute my love, please let me keep him,' the lovely lady rose and entreated her husband with big tear-filled eyes.

After what seemed like an eternity, Hades handed me over to his wife with a grunt and I breathed a sigh of relief, safe once more in her perfumed arms. 'Your mother is causing a bit of a problem on earth,' Hades said to Persephone. I hoped I wasn't going to witness a domestic argument.

The Secret Adventures of Rolo

'It seems she has gone on strike and if I don't release you from the Underworld then mankind will starve as she will not allow their crops to grow. I don't like being bullied by a woman and I don't know what all the fuss is about. Sort it out will you.' And with that he leapt on his chariot and left the hall in a hurry.

'May I speak?' I piped up.

Persephone set me on a low table and bent down to listen more closely.

'Speak little drakon,' she sighed.

'Don't you like it here? Does he treat you badly?' I asked.

'Well, I don't mind Hades himself – he has a softer side that nobody else sees. He's full of bluster to the outside world, but he can be kind in his own way. But I haven't been able to eat anything since I arrived here. I've completely lost my appetite. I don't want to be here all the time in this miserable place, it's like a dungeon and I do miss my mother.' She spoke softly.

'Well, why don't you strike a bargain? Stand up for yourself,' I ventured.

This seemed a novel idea in Ancient Greece. 'Why not see if your husband will let you return to earth for a certain time each year, on the understanding that you will return to spend an agreed amount of time with him in his lovely, erm, kingdom. How does that sound?'

'Clever little drakon, that is a marvellous solution!' Now all I have to do is persuade him. And only if he lets me keep you as a pet,' Persephone added, dabbing her beautiful eyes with a hanky.

Oh no! That's not part of the bargain. How am I going to get out of this one?

'I think I shall call you Derkomai.'

I didn't have to wonder for very long what that meant.

'You are the 'seeing one': you see an answer to my problem.'

Persephone patted me on the head as if I were a little dog and I must say she sounded a lot more cheerful than when I'd first entered the room.

'All of a sudden I feel hungry!' the beautiful young woman pulled a platter of fresh fruit towards her. I remembered Yulia's warning not to eat anything in the Underworld, but guessed it only applied to me. I watched spellbound as Persephone chose a pomegranate, tearing through the leathery skin and biting chunks of the fleshy fruit. Blood-coloured juice was running down her chin as she broke her sad fast, feasting on the bright red pips as if her life depended on it.

'Are you sure you won't have any? It's delicious,' she said, holding a piece of dripping fruit out to me. I resisted. To be fair, if it had been steak I might have been tempted.

Suddenly, Hades himself reappeared in the centre of the room. He had a helmet under his arm. I wondered how he did that – I certainly hadn't heard or seen him enter and there was no sign of the chariot.

'He's always coming and going,' she whispered in my ear, 'his helmet has magical properties – when worn both it and the wearer become invisible. It's a bit creepy to be honest.'

I wondered how much of our conversation he had heard.

'I think we have solved the problem.' Persephone explained the plan. Hades listened to his beautiful wife and conceded,

'Very well, you can spend eight months of the year with your mother and four months of the year down here with me in my realm. How does that sound? I don't want to make you unhappy, but I can't give you up entirely. Go at once to see your mother and persuade her to resume her duty of overseeing the crops and bring this drought to an end.'

'Make sure you look after Derkomai for me whilst I'm away,' she said over her shoulder as she skipped out of the draughty hall.

Now I had to manage my own escape. I quickly hatched a plan.

It was just the two of us, dragon and man. I asked Hades to tell me about life as a Greek god. As I had suspected, he loved talking about himself; there was no stopping him. Whilst he was telling me stories about Zeus, Poseidon and life on Mount Olympus and all the tricks they played on mankind, he drank deeply from a large silver goblet. I could tell he was getting sleepy and before long he was snoring loudly with his head slumped on his folded arms across the table.

I seized the moment, grabbed the helmet and pulled it over my head. It was so big I disappeared inside it. Literally – for I had become invisible.

I made for the exit and slipped unseen past Cerberus. The three headed dog was still having an argument with itself. I caught up with Persephone by the jetty. She was having a hard time persuading Charon to take her across to the other side of the river.

'I've forgotten my purse,' she wailed.

'I need to run this by the boss,' said Charon. 'My orders are that nothing leaves this place,' and the ferryman left her sitting in the ghostly boat whilst he went into the palace to find Hades.

I was still invisible under the helmet when I jumped on board the boat. I flung the helmet off and it fell with a clatter at Persephone's feet giving her the fright of her life when I appeared beside her.

'If I were you, I would grab that stick and punt us over to the other side,' I said, 'before that husband of yours changes his mind.'

Persephone didn't hesitate, picked up the pole and started pushing the boat out into the river. Charon reappeared shaking his fist.

And then the booming voice of Hades could be heard across the water. 'Farewell, my lovely. Your departure does not trouble me. I have found the remains of the pomegranate you ate and so am assured of your return.'

Little had Persephone realised that by eating a few fruit pips and thereby breaking her fast in the Underworld, Hades had a hold on her for evermore. Poor Persephone! Her destiny was sealed. Mental note to self: never touch a pomegranate!

I stayed around to watch the very moving reunion of mother and daughter on the opposite river bank. In front of my eyes I could see seeds starting to germinate and green shoots pushing up through the bare earth: the drought was finally over, spring was on its way.

I thought about Persephone having to return to the Underworld and understood that this is why Ancient Greeks believed that nature dies back in winter when Demeter is mourning the loss of her daughter, but that Hades keeping his pledge to let Persephone return to her mother every year, assured the fertile time of spring and the promise of a good harvest to come.

I wondered for a fleeting moment how Charon was going to get his ferry back. At least I'd left Hades' helmet on-board – much as I knew the floppy haired boy would enjoy testing its invisibility powers, I knew Athelstan wouldn't let me keep it as it belonged in mythology not modern day.

'Can you get the jewel collar off me please, my wings are tired and I'm dying to scratch,' I begged Yulia once I had arrived back at the foot of the oak tree.

'Had enough dragon adventure for one night, Little Pup?' smiled Athelstan. I couldn't wait to feel the tingling sensation as my dragon scales turned back into fur and my scaly legs once more became paws.

'I'll take care of this then,' said Yulia, as she climbed down inside the tree roots with the collar.

Rolodogblog #9 #retailtherapy

The smiley lady has an old friend to stay. She could be the twin of the smiley lady; they are the same age, height and build. The only difference really is that the old friend has a northern accent.

That's not to say the friend is old — what I mean is the smiley lady and northern twin have known each other since they were students. I can't get a word in edgeways. They are chattering away nineteen

to the dozen, rolling back
the years and giggling like
schoolgirls. I bring my squeaky
toys to get some attention but they
just take them off me and put them
out of reach and go back to their
reminiscing, occasionally dishing
out absent-minded pats without
really taking any notice of me.
This is not much fun at all.

The twins decide to go clothes
shopping. This is dangerous because
there is a sale on in the shop they
both love and they are putting
lipstick on and colourful scarves
over their coats — and, phew, the
smiley lady picks up my lead.

Always a good sign. So I am not
going to be left at home. We walk
along the High Street. Everyone
admires me. I am so handsome and

such a good boy.

I know which shop they are heading
for because I am welcome in there.
Mistral. The manageress keeps
a pot of doggy biscuits for me
(well probably for other dogs
too). I pull the twins inside
and am greeted by name and more
importantly with biscuits. I am

happy. The twins are oohing and aahing over the greatly reduced colourful items hanging on the sale rails. My lead is handed to a sales assistant who makes a great fuss of me and feeds me more biscuits. I am content. The twins disappear into the changing rooms at the back of the shop. I hear,

'Does my bottom look big in this?' from one. I couldn't possibly comment.

'Does it bring anything to the party? If not, put it back and walk away' — this from the smiley lady who would do well to heed her own advice.

There are clothes piled on the counter. I am bored now.

'Come on, twins, walk away from
the sale rails — pay and exit the
shop,' I wanted to say.

The smiley lady bought a new
raincoat that wasn't even in the
sale! It's bright yellow and she
looks like a deep-sea fisherman;
all she needs is a sou'wester. Her
northern twin says it's her colour
and she looks wonderful in it. I'm
sniggering behind my paw.
At last we are back out in the
fresh air of the High Street. There
are lots of wee mails to check
on various lamp posts and corners
and crumbs to hoover, especially
outside the take-away bakers. We
head home dodging the rain.
Bored with women's chit chat and
shopping, I crave adventure.

#rolohatesshopping

Chapter 11

Rolo and Aesop's Fables

The floppy haired boy is reading Aesop's Fables. This is a collection of short moral tales thought to have been created by a slave called Aesop in Ancient Greece somewhere between 650 and 564 BC. This storyteller used animals as characters in his stories to get his simple messages across. None of the characters are named; they are simply called The Wolf, The Fox, The Crane, The Goat and so on.

The floppy haired boy is lying on his bed leaning on his hands and deeply engrossed in the stories. He hasn't put the stair gate up so I am assuming I am allowed to venture to the great upstairs and into the boy cave.

I creep in quietly so as not to disturb him and then put my front paws up on his bed and lean back, wagging my tail and looking at him appealingly. The trick works and he pats the duvet next to him and goes straight back to his book.

'You're lucky mum's out, Rolo, or you wouldn't be allowed up here. But you know that don't you, clever boy.'

Actually, what I do know is that I like human company, and to tunnel under the duvet where I feel safe and warm as if I were in a fox hole – when I can get away with it! The floppy haired boy is usually a soft touch.

'You'll like this one, Rolo,' he said, and started to read aloud:

'A Dog, to whom the butcher had thrown a bone, was hurrying home with his prize as fast as he could go. As he crossed a narrow bridge, he happened to look down and saw himself reflected in the still water as if in a mirror. But the greedy Dog thought he saw another Dog carrying a bone much bigger than his own.

'If he had stopped to think he would have known better. But instead of thinking, he dropped his bone

and sprang at the Dog in the river, only to find himself swimming for dear life to reach the shore. At last he managed to scramble out, and as he stood sadly thinking about the good bone he had lost, he realised what a stupid Dog he had been.'

And the moral of this tale is 'It is very foolish to be greedy' – okay, Rolo, have you got that?'

Well, I thought this was rather silly. I would have put my bone down safely on the bank before jumping in to take the bigger bone off the river dog, but, well, it's just a story.

'Here's another one.' The floppy haired boy shared

the tale of The Cockerel and the Jewel with me:

'A Cockerel was busily scratching and scraping to find something to eat for himself and his family. He happened to turn up a precious jewel that had been lost by its owner.

"'Aha!" said the Cockerel. "No doubt you are very costly and he who lost you would give a great deal to find you. But as for me, I would choose a single grain of barleycorn before all the jewels in the world."'

I put my head on one side waiting to hear the moral.

'And here's the punch line, Rolo,' continued the floppy haired boy. 'Precious things are without value to those who cannot prize them.'

He closed the book and went downstairs. I followed, hoping for a treat if he was going anywhere near the biscuit tin. I was rewarded with a dog biscuit in the shape of a bone whilst he tucked into a few chocolate ones. Just as well the smiley lady was out. I curled up in my basket and he went out on his skateboard. That last fable got me thinking – what if the jewel in the fable was the one from my collar? Supposing I was actually visiting Aesop in Ancient Greece in my dragon form and somehow lost the jewel? How would I get back to present times and how could I turn back into Rolo the lovable Jack Russell without it?

Here's an idea: Aesop and I are in the hen house and he makes up the story and during the telling of it, with me and the hens as rapt listeners, somehow the jewel becomes loose and falls on the floor.

This mishap goes unnoticed by the broody hens that are all sleepy on their roosts, but it is seen by the clever Cockerel whose bright beady eye spies the sparkling jewel lying there amongst the straw.

The Cockerel tucks it away for safe keeping. Aesop and I move on to another location and weave another story, oblivious to the fact that I have lost the jewel and the consequences thereof.

When I realise that the jewel is missing I run back to the hen house with a whole sack of barleycorn to bargain with the Cockerel, because that jewel is worth so much to me and nothing at all to him.

My mind was reeling and my imagination was working overtime! I longed to make up my own fable. The floppy haired boy said that was what people did these days – they used the original format of setting a scene and animals to describe some of the action and then reached a conclusion backed up by a thought-provoking message.
So here goes then…

A Jack Russell is out chasing rabbits in the wild and, before long, he realised that he had wandered far and is lost. Sniffing about here and there trying to find a familiar trail he spies a Panther with a hungry look on his face.

The Jack Russell thinks, 'Oh, dear! I'm in deep

trouble now!'

He sees some bones on the ground and at once crouches over them with his back to the stealthy Panther. The Panther coils a short distance away and is about to spring on his lunch when the wily Jack Russell smacks his lips noisily, burps and says out loud,

'That was such a tasty Panther. I wonder where I can find another one for dessert.'

When this outburst reaches the hungry Panther's ears he diverts his leap and instead slinks off into the wood.

The panther says out loud, 'Golly! That was a near thing! I nearly ended up as the Jack Russell's lunch!'

Overhead in the tree a Monkey is watching this pantomime and plans how he can use it to his advantage.

The Monkey chases after the hungry Panther and tells him what he saw in exchange for the promise of protection from the Panther.

The Panther listens and is angry about being fooled by the Jack Russell and made to look silly in front of the Monkey, so he tells the Monkey to jump on his back so he can witness how he will take revenge on the Jack Russell.

The wily Jack Russell sees the sly Monkey riding the hungry Panther coming straight for him.

'Uh-oh! I'm for it now! Time for some quick thinking.'

Instead of instinctively scarpering as fast as his paws can carry him, the Jack Russell sits with his back to the nearing Panther. When he is sure they are within earshot, he says out loud:

'I wonder where that sly Monkey has got to. I sent him off a while ago to bring me another Panther for pudding.'

And the moral of my fable?

'A quick- witted Jack Russell will outsmart even the scariest animal.'

Mmm… not bad if I say so myself. Shame I can't share this self-penned fable with the floppy haired boy.

Rolodogblog #10 #scouts #hedgehogs
There is always a bonfire put on

by the Scouts as a community event every year round about 5th November to remember Guy Fawkes.

Oh yes, I remember him well enough — I met him in Book 3 and stopped him blowing up king and parliament back in the 17th century. As you may recall, I don't like fireworks — they make me angry, so the smiley lady and floppy haired boy never take me to the bonfire. We stay indoors with the television turned up very loudly indeed to disguise all the loud bangs.

The bonfire had been built since the middle of October, with the scouts adding branches from their gardens and neighbouring hedges — all neatly stacked like a tepee ready for the big night.

The smiley lady was very concerned that small furry creatures and not so furry creatures — like hedgehogs — might be hibernating in the warmth and safety of the stacked woodpile and were at risk of being toasted when the bonfire was lit. She rang the scoutmaster. I heard her telling the floppy haired boy that she was taking me down to the scout hut grounds to do a 'hedgehog sweep'. This sounded like a fun game!

What it actually entailed was me being paraded in a circle around the stacked wood on my lead to alert the scouts if there was any wildlife present before they lit the fire.

I performed my job very well. I understood what was expected of me.

I could report that no animals —
furry or spikey — were present in
the wood pile, and the scout leader
made me the honorary mascot of the
troop and asked the smiley lady if
she would bring me back next year
to perform the same exercise.

#roloisprepared
#rolowouldliketomeetBearGrylls

Chapter 12

Gwyn lost

We were on our way to see Grandad Polo, driving along that very long road called the M4, but in the opposite direction to Wales. The smiley lady was singing along to the radio as usual and trying her best at the morning pop quiz, shouting out the answers as if the contestant on the radio could hear her.

I looked out the window and saw trucks and cars and trees and strips of green fields lining either side of the big noisy carriageway. It was raining and I could see drops of water racing down the windows. The windscreen wipers were swooshing frantically from side to side trying to keep the window clear. Watching them made me drowsy like I was being hypnotised. I nodded off, secure in my travelling cage on the back seat, lulled by the sound.

Just before we turn off for Grandad's, about an hour into the journey, we usually pass a field with horses. Nothing unusual about that you might think, but these are small white horses, about a dozen of them, all the same size and all the same colour; they look like part of the landscape because they are always there, throughout the year whatever the weather, just standing around in a field.

'No horses today,' said the smiley lady, presumably to me, as we came off the motorway at the right junction. I peered out of the rain-lashed side window and saw she was quite correct; an empty field. No sign of the small white horses. I didn't think any more about it.

We visited Grandad Polo and I played blinking games with him and hoovered him for crumbs after he'd eaten the smiley lady's rock cakes. When I'd been admired by the carers and other residents, I was bundled back in the car and we headed home.

The rain had stopped but the sun was stubbornly refusing to shine. Everything was glistening wet and the cars threw up lots of spray either side of their wheels and the water lay in deep puddles in places along the gutters. I could tell by the way the smiley lady was hunched over the steering wheel that she didn't enjoy driving in these weather conditions.

As we re-joined the motorway, I glanced across the central reservation and beyond it to the other side of the carriageway. Still no white horses in the field. That night Yulia came a-tapping on the kitchen window. I was in a deep sleep dreaming about bounding across spring meadows, chasing rabbits. It was rather a sudden awakening and I stumbled over to the trapdoor, stretching forward and back like the yoga expert that I am, and opened the secret door with my teeth.

'Wakey-wakey, Paddy Paws! Athelstan needs you!'

The woodland girl seemed quite agitated. It had been a while since I was last summoned, so I threw off the drowsy warmth of sleep by having a good shake and joined her in the cold night air of the back garden.

'What's the problem, Yulia?' I asked.

'Athelstan will tell you,' she replied.

'It's Gwyn,' said the tree dragon when I stood before him, all ears.

'He's disappeared. He's never done that before.'

Yulia and Da shuffled about uncomfortably staring intently at the leaf mould under their feet and wouldn't look Athelstan in the eye. Neither of the woodland folk was going to volunteer any information, so it was up to yours truly to tell the truth.

'Actually he has,' I said quietly.

'WHAT?' roared Athelstan, shaking the leaves of his oak tree.

Yulia rolled her eyes at me and then spoke up,

'A few months ago Gwyn tested his wings, went for an outing and got a bit lost, that's all. Paddy Paws had to go and retrieve him,' she said quietly.

'Why didn't I know about this?' fumed Athelstan.

Poor Yulia was quaking in her little green shoes and Da was just standing there harrumphing so I came to her defence,

'They didn't want to bother you, Athelstan, and anyway no harm was done – I simply had to go and fetch him.'

'And how did you do that?'

'Erm, with the help of a pair of red kites,' I finished lamely. I could see Athelstan's eye getting rounder and bigger as the enormity of the cover up was revealed to him.

'In that case it's quite possible that he has taken himself off for another test flight,' said Athelstan, 'maybe we don't need to worry quite so much but I would like you to find him. Probably best if you go in dragon mode. Are you up for that? And you two, you're both grounded. You can stay here in the forest and dust the bluebells or something.'

Yulia disappeared down a hole behind the large tree root and came back with my jewel collar.

'You're going to need this then if you are to be Rodor. I doubt Gwyn has gone too far; he will be around here somewhere. Easier to find a dragon if you are a dragon yourself, I suppose.'

Yulia looked a little bit crestfallen and I knew it wasn't really her fault. Gwyn was growing fast and a lively young dragon was too much for a couple of small woodland folk to keep tabs on. There was a size issue for a start! Gwyn was more manageable when he was newly hatched, but now he was bigger it was quite impossible.

I nudged Yulia with my nose and it had the desired

effect – she giggled, and then got into position
perched on the root to attach the jewel collar around
my neck. Athelstan still seemed to be sulking and
wasn't giving out any clues as to where I should look
first, so I needed to think where might be a good
place to start my search for a missing dragon.

I had the strangest feeling that someone was
watching me. I couldn't really put my paw on it and
none of the others seemed aware of anything being
amiss. I must be imagining things and put it out of
my mind better to concentrate on the task.

When the buckle was fastened and the collar
turned so that the jewel was under my chin, Yulia
stepped away and I felt the now familiar sensation
of my body turning from fur into scales, dog into
dragon. I glanced down at my paws and noted with
satisfaction that they were claws, and a swish of
my tail confirmed that it was arrow tipped rather
than the white tipped flag which usually wagged
at will. I was ready. I went from standing still to
running fast in nought to three seconds and as my

strides lengthened I felt the earth beneath me giving way and before you could say 'Jack Russell' I was airborne.

Up over the tree tops and high in the sky and…then where? I had absolutely no idea where I was going or where to start looking for the missing dragon. Last time Gwyn did this he didn't venture very far, but it was anyone's guess where he might be this time.

I heard a familiar keening cry as I soared through the low cloud and glancing down I saw Jory and Milva, the red kites, riding the thermals just below me presumably on a hunting mission. I swooped low towards them but they were startled and looked as if they wanted to attack me – of course, I'd forgotten, last time they saw me I was a dog – they didn't recognise me at all!

'Jory, Milva, it's Roro!' I called out, hoping they could hear me as they were gliding with the current. Milva was swooping in for the kill when Jory called out and managed to deflect her when he suddenly

The Secret Adventures of Rolo

realised who I was, although I couldn't explain
my strange appearance whilst I was concentrating
on flying. The three of us dove down to earth and
alighted in a field away from people.

'Roro! I nearly killed you!' said Milva. 'What on
earth have you done to yourself?'

I explained to the birds about the jewel collar and
my ability to turn into a dragon and they looked
suitably impressed.

'Well, you're the second dragon we've seen today,'
said Jory and my heart leapt.

'The other one was white and a bit bigger than you.
I thought I recognised him as the young scamp who
had invaded our nest a while back,' he added.

'Yes, that sounds like Gwyn! Do you know where he
was heading?'

'No idea, but his wings looked a good deal stronger

than when we last saw him.'

'How are your babies?' I asked politely.

'Oh, they've all flown the nest now,' said Milva proudly, but I detected a note of sadness in her voice.

'I've just thought of something that might help you in your search, Roro,' said Jory.

'Yesterday when we flew over the big hill south west of here, we heard a bit of a commotion coming from within. No idea what it was and we didn't go down to investigate as there was a storm approaching. Your wandering dragon may have gone there.'

'Can you show me where it is?'

'Of course, follow us!'

We took to the air once more and, after a short distance, alighted at the foot of the big hill not too

far from the forest, as the dragon or kite flies.
I recognised it at once as Silbury Hill; the smiley
lady said it was a mystical mound that had been
constructed several thousand years ago and that
nobody knew its purpose.

It had been excavated several times during the last
couple of centuries, but not the tiniest fragment of
human or animal bone, not even bits of pottery have
ever been found in the earth. That was all I knew.
I strained my dragon ears to pick up any sound and
had to admit I couldn't hear anything at all coming
from within the big hill.

Circling round the top, which was somewhat sunken
due to poorly planned excavations in past years, I
noticed what looked a bit like a plug hole.

My jewel collar started to burn around my neck and
I wanted to ask the kites if they could peck it off,
but then I thought if I landed and this did turn out
to be a wild goose chase, I would have no means of
continuing my search by air or, more importantly, of

getting back home.

To my amazement the plug hole in the top of the hill slid to one side and I found myself peering down a giant hole. It was dark inside even though the jewel on my collar was throwing out a ghostly glow of light. Despite being a dragon, my natural terrier shake started up involuntarily; although I was scared, I felt compelled to go in.

The Secret Adventures of Rolo

Chapter 13

Rolo and the Unicorns

Jory and Milva were hovering anxiously overhead, flapping their wings to stay airborne. Jory wanted to follow me, but as I descended into the hole the grass covering slid back across the top of it barring his entry or indeed my exit.

Well, that's it. I'm now inside the big hill with no visible means of escape!

There was nothing else for it but to fly down to the base of the vault to find out what was going on. I steadied my wings and floated towards the ground and then picked out a strange sound – a sort of whickering – which grew louder and more anxious as I got nearer.

I could just about make out a sea of white below me and thought I was going to land on a cushion of clouds or soft marshmallow, but ouch! – No soft landing – I hit a spike, collided with another spike and then found myself lying on my back on the floor, surrounded by a whole lot of rather menacing pointy things. Had I landed on a giant albino hedgehog?

My eyes tuned into the darkness with the jewel helping to illuminate the scene. I could not believe my eyes – unicorns! About a dozen of them, surrounding me with their spiralled horns angled down rather like knights dipping their lances at the start of a joust.

I wasted no time in addressing them,

'Greetings all! I am Rodor. I'm looking for a small white dragon. Have you seen him? He's a bit bigger than me and not great with words?'

The unicorns backed away a bit to give me some room and suddenly I didn't feel quite so threatened. I sat up and put my back legs through my front ones – more Rolo than Rodor.

'I've never seen a unicorn before and here you are in

a herd – or what is it you call a group of unicorns? I'm rather interested in collective nouns.' I couldn't help babbling nonsense in my excitement.

'I think it should be a 'unity of unicorns'. I wish the floppy haired boy could see you! You look a bit familiar, I don't know why…' I tailed off and tried to collect my thoughts. I was feeling a bit star struck – it's not every day you get to meet a unicorn!

'What are you all doing in here anyway?' I asked. A general murmuring started up. One stepped forward and shook his mane for silence.

The spokes-unicorn of the group introduced himself as Sigil and explained,

The Secret Adventures of Rolo

'We look like ordinary horses by day. It's only in secret and when no humans are around that we change into unicorns and...' He broke off when he heard mutterings of alarm from the others.

'It's okay, everyone. I feel we can trust this little dragon. Rodor, I will tell you our secret as I hope you can help us escape from this place.'

Sigil paused, gave a look of reassurance to his fellow unicorns and then said,

'Once a year in the dead of night we fly south-west from our field to a chalk white horse on a hill. Here we hold an ancient ritual.'

I could feel my eyes widening to the size of doggy bowls at this revelation! I nodded, impressed but trying to keep my excitement reined in.

'I've seen those chalk horses on the Downs – I've always wondered if they were magical!' I whispered. The leader of the unicorns continued,

'Yesterday was the date for our annual ceremony
– the vital recharging of our magical powers, that
of invisibility and transformation between horse
and unicorn. Night came and we assembled at the
appointed time and place as usual ready to place our
front left hoof on the imprint of the chalk horse, the
key source of our powers.'

I had visions of them doing the hokey cokey on the
hillside and tried to suppress the urge to giggle. Sigil
went on,

'This is top secret of course. We have never told any
of this to anyone before, but now we are being held
captive and are desperate to be free. Do you think
you can help us?'

241

'I will try, but tell me first how you were captured,' I said.

'We were on the point of starting our ceremony when a small man in a tall battered hat and dark clothing arrived at the chalk white horse. We were shocked to have a witness though were thankful to still be in our horse disguise. He took advantage of our surprise and our powers being at their weakest and rounded us up with halter ropes, which he threw skilfully around our necks before bundling us into a big trailer. We had never seen him before and were so stunned we were unable to resist. The man said he was taking us to the Mythical Domain where we could be unicorns all the time and not just secretly. This shocked us as we can't imagine how he knew our secret. Now you find us frightened and upset because we are losing our special powers by the minute, and we are imprisoned here without any means of escape.'

'What are your names?' I asked, remembering my manners. They already knew who I was.

Sigil pointed to each in turn as he told me what they were called.

'This is Estar with a star on her head, Sable with a black streak, Roshan with apple cheeks, Silvesse with a silver mane, Arryn with a snowflake pattern on his back, Helios with a sun spot, Erwyn with a silver hoof, Elmas with a grey tail, Jaden with rounded ears and Jonty with freckles.'

'But aren't there twelve of you?' I queried, counting on my claws.

Looking distressed, Silvesse explained,

'The man kept hold of Rune's halter as he undid the trailer at the foot of the hill and told us if we didn't obey him and run to the top and jump into the Domain we would never see our brother again. We were all denying we were unicorns of course, pretending to be just ordinary horses. We involuntarily changed into unicorns on entering the hill – it must have its own magical properties.'

The Secret Adventures of Rolo

'The man didn't come in with you?' I asked.

'No, he kept hold of Rune and stayed outside and then the roof closed over us,' said freckled Jonty, shaking his head sadly.

Hmmm, I wondered who this animal thief could be and why he had stolen the horses, and whether he knew they were really unicorns.

All this drama with the captives had distracted me from my mission to find Gwyn. I asked them when they had heard him.

'Just before you arrived I heard something on the outside, making a strange noise that sounded like 'Roro' and I must admit I hoped Roro would be some kind of superhero coming to our aid not a small tri-coloured dragon. No offence to you of course,' said Sigil.

None taken, I thought to myself. I'll let that one go. It must have been Gwyn! If he was calling my name he must have sensed trouble.

'Sorry we can't be much help, but our powers are drained. If we don't escape tonight we will lose our chance to boost them!' said Sigil sadly.

'If I can get you out of here can you get yourselves back to your field?' I asked.

'We will need to go back via the white horse to recharge our powers first, and it has to be tonight or we won't be able to change into horses anymore and we will remain unicorns forever,' Sigil said.

I flew to the top of the vault, wondering if my jewel collar might activate the exit just like the pink orb opens the time tunnel, but no such luck. I was banging my head against a grass covered roof. It didn't budge. Not from the inside anyway. This was not going to work.

OK Rodor, think, I said to myself. What would Athelstan do? And then it came to me.

'Can you help me get the jewel collar off?' I asked, as I flew back down to the unicorns gathered on the floor of the vault.

Sigil and Erwin used their pointy horns to unfasten my collar and the circle of unicorns drew back in astonishment as I turned from dragon into small dog in front of their eyes. It was quite a party trick and I thought they would be impressed – but on reflection maybe not – after all they could switch between horse and unicorn when their powers were working properly. I couldn't help myself; I had to use a back leg to scratch behind my ear. I could hear horsey sniggering. Yeah, I bet you can't do that with your hooves, I thought rather childishly.

'What escape plan do you have in mind, Rodor?' enquired Sigil.

'Small point,' I began, 'when I'm a dog I'm called Rolo – unless you are a young dragon who can't say 'Rolo' properly hence 'Roro'. I'm only Rodor when I am a dragon, so technically it's Rolo right now.' The unicorns looked at me blankly.

'Oh, never mind… how are your kicking skills?' I asked uncertainly – their hooves looked a bit too dainty and refined for any heavy work.

I went over to the turf wall at the base of the chamber and started tunnelling as we terriers do best: scraping madly at the mud with my front paws and flicking it away behind me. Once I'd made an impression in the wall I stepped out of the way and the unicorns went at the dent, kicking away with their hooves, two at a time. Very soon they had made a hole through the thick earth and a rush of air confirmed we had broken through to the outside. It was just large enough to fit a Jack Russell through at any rate. I wriggled through on my tummy, propelling myself forward.

Out in the fresh air I wasted no time in running to the top of the hill, carrying the jewel collar in my teeth. I was banking on the jewel collar acting as some kind of remote control to open the top of the hill from the outside thus allowing the unicorns to escape and complete their ritual. My theory worked and the hill opened.

I had already briefed the unicorns that if the roof opened they were to fly out at once, but they didn't want to leave without their brother. We were losing time.

Suddenly I heard the beating of wings overhead and looked up to see young Gwyn beaming from ear to ear and making straight for me feet first.

He came in to land right on top of me, knocking me off my feet and almost back into the hole. I tried to explain about the captive unicorns, but I could sense he wasn't really getting it. He kept saying Roro and nuzzling me. Before the unicorns had a chance to react I heard the beating of more wings approaching and to my amazement a unicorn alighted on the other side of the hole, being ridden by a small stubby man wearing a battered top hat and a long dark coat. The man was chuckling to himself and rubbing his hands with glee as he dismounted, keeping the unicorn's reins hooked over the crook of his arm.

This must be the missing Rune. The poor unicorn looked very distressed and whispered to me,

'I was trying to escape by turning into a unicorn. I didn't mean to give our secret away but thought if I sacrificed myself I could save the others. I think he's a collector of some sort,' Rune added, hanging his head, his spiral horn pointing to the ground.

The man in the top hat had set his beady eyes on Gwyn and was advancing toward him, gurgling with delight, his hands outstretched. He was tripping over his long coat.

'So, I have a herd of unicorns for my Domain and now I spy a white dragon – get away you mutt!' He lashed out at me with his foot.

'I don't have any need for a common dog in my collection. Mythical creatures only,' he rasped.

249

Little do you know you ignoramus! I thought to myself.

'I will trade you my white dragon for your unicorn,' I spoke up, pushing Gwyn towards him. That worked! The man spun round and gave me his full attention, 'Well, well, a talking dog! Now that IS quite magical!' he said with a glint in his eye.

I could see the way his mind was working. He was now thinking how he could have all the unicorns and the dragon and the talking dog for his collection, but boy had he underestimated this Jack Russell.

'Go ahead, take the unicorn, I've another eleven in there. I'll swap him for the dragon,' he smiled and offered me poor Rune's reins.

I shoved Gwyn towards the gaping hole and hoped that the unicorns inside had been listening to our conversation and knew that their brother had returned.

Gwyn looked horrified at this exchange and reluctantly entered the hill prison. Rune was standing forlornly next to me. I nuzzled in closer to give him encouragement.

'How did you manage to open the roof?' the man demanded.

I certainly wasn't going to tell him about my jewel collar.

We were interrupted by a familiar keening sound, heralding the approach of birds of prey. I knew immediately who it was – Jory and Milva. They must have been watching this exchange, as they flew directly at the collector and pecked and swooped at him menacingly until he tripped over the hem of his coat and fell into the hole; they went in after him. I heard human yelps of pain as he must have landed on several upturned unicorn horns whilst being bitten along the way.

The next arrival on the scene was Rhydian the Welsh dragon.

'Quick, Ci Em, we don't have much time. Athelstan
sends this message. Listen carefully, all of you,'
he boomed – he didn't even land. The red dragon
recited loudly as he flapped his wings, managing to
hover over the hole as his voice rang out to reach the
captives inside the hill,

'If fourteen creatures rise,
They can leave the Domain and take to the skies.
Red and white they are all on the wing,
Unicorns, dragon, and birds that don't sing.'

I had no idea what it meant. But his words had the
desired effect on the unicorns.

Suddenly there was a tremendous commotion
from within the hill and the unicorns rose, spilling
out like white volcanic ash, dispersing in different
directions. This must have taken all their remaining
strength. I hoped for their sakes that the chalk white
horse they needed to get to was located nearby.
The momentum of their escape brought Gwyn up to
the surface with them and out he popped like a cork

from a bottle of fizz. He landed beside me and Rune took off at once to join his family. Finally, the red kites swooped out; they didn't hang around and were quickly on their way.

The Secret Adventures of Rolo

So, Athelstan's rhyme was a prophesy. The unicorns were free with the collector now captive inside the hill.

I scampered down the grassy bank with Gwyn at my tail. It was my theory that if I moved far enough away from the top with my jewel collar the roof would close, and sure enough it did.

'We've got him trapped,' I shouted triumphantly.

My glee was short-lived as I suddenly remembered the hole we had made at the bottom of the hill, big enough for a terrier but too small for unicorns. My fear was that it might just be large enough for a small man if he slithered on his tummy.

Quickly I raced around to block the exit, but alas I was too late. The collector had already crawled out and was standing at the base of the hill. I barked at him. He ignored me and started making a strange whistling sound, sending it out into the night air. Gwyn just stood there, rooted to the spot.

A rustling sound meant something was approaching fast. I looked up thinking it might be another dragon, but the swooshing of wings was softer, more like feathers. I wondered if one of the kites had returned, but, no, it was a very large and colourful bird, with incandescent plumage finished off with a sheen of shimmering gold and silver giving the illusion that the bird was on fire. Gwyn stared as if in a trance.

The unusual bird landed beside the collector who climbed straight on its back and, in the blink of an eye, the glorious creature took off and raced into the velvet night encouraged by its stumpy rider shouting, 'Away, phoenix, away!'

Last thing I saw was the silhouette of the phoenix with its distinctive tail feathers trailing, flying across the moon with the top-hatted collector urging it on as if racing the final furlong of the Grand National. I could just make out two more winged creatures on the horizon and the phoenix and its rider were heading in their direction. I couldn't be sure, but screwing my eyes up, it looked very much like they were chasing dragons.

'Time to go home, Ci Em,' said Rhydian and he waited patiently with Gwyn, expecting me to transform myself back into a dragon for the short flight home.

The unicorns were now dots flying eastwards in formation.

I was still very much a small dog. I looked down to
see furry paws and wagged my tail in frustration.

'Where is the jewel collar?' I said in dismay,
searching around on the ground where I had been
standing. Gwyn and Rhydian joined in the hunt.

We combed the grass, top and bottom of the hill,
but the jewel collar was nowhere to be seen. The
roof had closed and the Domain was sealed. Maybe
it was still inside? I went to the hole at the base and
scrambled inside the hill but couldn't see a thing
in the pitch dark. I called Rhydian and he breathed
gentle fire through the hole to illuminate the interior
but to no avail. There was no sign of the collar and
without it I could not transform from dog to dragon.

'I don't think it's here. It must be lost. Come on,
Ci Em, let us not waste any more time in fruitless
search. I will give you a ride,' said Rhydian, when
I returned outside empty-pawed, and the dragon
obligingly lowered his tail as a ramp towards the
hole to ease my clambering onto his neck.

Gwyn flew quietly alongside us and in no time at all we three were back at the foot of the Athelstan tree in the forest.

If Athelstan was surprised to see me as a dog astride the Welsh dragon, his woody features didn't give anything away. He must have been pleased to see Gwyn safely returned. I told the guardian of the time tunnel that I was very sorry but that I seemed to have mislaid the jewel collar.

Athelstan answered in a riddle,

'The changing one is chosen;
He can enter the tree.
You had to work together to set the unicorns free.
Adventure again will be what you seek;
When creatures are contained, the world is bleak.
But know that freedom is never free;
There is a price as you will see.'

And that was all he would say before he disappeared. I was too tired to think about the meaning of all this. Feeling a bit disappointed, I bade goodnight to the two dragons and took myself home seeking the comfort of my basket, hoping to snatch some sleep before morning.

I'd left it a bit late as the inky night was already retreating and dawn's rosy glow was creeping from the eastern horizon heralding a new day. It did cross my mind that one of these mornings after an action-packed adventure I might not actually make it back to the kitchen before sunrise!

The smiley lady thought I was a bit off colour when she opened the kitchen door a few hours later.

'Must be something Rolo's eaten, he's not quite himself today,' she said to the floppy haired boy and they both smothered me with lots of cuddles. I didn't mind that. But I couldn't help feeling a bit let down by this latest adventure. With the disappearance of the jewel collar, did this mean I couldn't be a dragon anymore, or explore any more myths and legends?

Later that day the smiley lady and floppy haired boy encouraged me into my traveling cage on the back seat of the car and we set off along the familiar route to visit Grandad Polo.

I was still tired from the previous night's adventure and dozed off dreaming of all the experiences I'd recently had: the Bronze Age village, the founding of the United Arab Emirates, the end of the Trojan Wars, football in the trenches during World War One, the Cardiff dragon, the Underworld – they all started to blend into one. The aroma of freshly baked rock cakes filled the car reminding me of King Alfred. How could I have forgotten about meeting him!

The clicking of the indicator and change of engine sound made me realise we were nearly there as we left the motorway. Instinctively I glanced over to the field on my left. Sure enough, there were twelve small white horses standing around minding their own business.

The smiley lady pointed them out to the floppy haired boy and he noticed that one of them had a halter rope around its neck.

'That shows they are being exercised then,' she said. 'I thought they were just put out to pasture,' and she focused her attention back on the road.

I smiled a secret smile and snuggled down in my cage.

'If only you knew,' I thought to myself, happy to see them as horses and to know they must have reached the chalk white horse in time to have successfully changed back from unicorns.

Grandad Polo was reading a newspaper when we found him in his sunlit room.

He pointed out an interesting snippet to the floppy haired boy, who read it out loud to his mum,

'An exotic and rare bird has been sighted on

the Welsh border hovering over the ruins of Montgomery Castle. No one knows what species it is because every time someone gets near enough to identify it, the bird disappears. Reports say it is quite large and has flashy plumage of many colours and long curling tail feathers.'

'How exciting!' said the smiley lady, 'I wonder what it could be?' Grandad Polo used to enjoy a bit of bird watching.

'It sounds like a phoenix to me,' he said quietly.

'But they're not real, Grandad, only mythical,' said the floppy haired boy, exchanging glances with the smiley lady. I waited patiently for the tin of rock cakes to be opened, with my back legs folded carefully through my front legs.

'Look, Grandad, Rolo's doing 'clown eyes',' laughed the floppy haired boy.

I kept my torrent of thoughts to myself.

Chapter 14

Rolo to the Rescue

The following weekend the smiley lady put an overnight bag in the boot of the car, bundled me in my traveling cage and we set off.

'Don't forget to look out for the phoenix!' the floppy haired boy smiled as he waved us off. He already had his skateboard in hand and was heading off to stay with his friend overnight.

The car journey took several hours and I woke up as my cage was being opened, delighted to see that we had arrived at the home of the cheery cook. She feeds me titbits when the smiley lady isn't looking, and lets me sit on the sofas.

I was fussed over and then soon forgotten as the friends settled to easy chatter, catching up with each other's news.

I hung around the back door and the cheery cook finally noticed and let me out into the back garden.

My luck was in: another Jack Russell had been to stay – the cheery cook's sister has one called Todd – and he had rather obligingly dug an escape hole under the fence.

I had to get up to the castle. I felt sure that that was where the collector was hiding out – given away by the sighting of the phoenix.

Next door's garden had an open gate so I slipped out easily and crossed the road carefully, squeezed under the stile and followed the footpath across the field near the disused fox covet.

I selected a hole to descend and followed the earthy scent deep underground, remembering the way through the abandoned lair to the web of secret chambers beneath the castle ruin.

Listening carefully before I went into the first chamber, I could hear stamping and shuffling of feet coming from the second room. It didn't sound human. I peered into the gloom and edged in.

To my utter amazement, I saw Reod and Alba chained to a wall on short leashes.

The question was how to free them? I kept myself hidden whilst I thought of a plan. I didn't want to give my presence away to these two as the element of surprise was always a good thing in a rescue.

Glancing around the first chamber I saw a spluttering candle stub and a roll of bedding, a packet of biscuits, pair of binoculars, battered top hat and a rucksack stashed on one of the ledges. This must be where the collector had been hiding out. The man was nowhere to be seen though – perhaps out on reconnaissance for other creatures to join Reod and Alba in his Mythical Domain or whatever he called it. Or perhaps he was trying to round up the unicorns again.

A strange bird-like sound could be heard coming from a tall shaft leading off another underground chamber. I wondered if it was the phoenix. I didn't know what they sounded like. It didn't sound very happy and was possibly being held captive too. How on earth was I going to get in there and free it? That was some collection the man was trying to assemble – unicorns, dragons and a phoenix!

I needed some help and remembered Jory telling me that the red kites had a communication system set up so they could relay messages the length and breadth of the country. It was worth a try.

I scampered out from the chamber unobserved by the captive dragons and popped back out through the fox hole. I ran all the way up the hill to the ruins, past the information boards.

Luckily there were no humans around as it was a dismal day. I used a previously untested tactic – I played dead, rolling on my back with my feet in the air, closing my eyes tight and hoping that I could lure the birds of prey down and then reveal myself, before they thought I was a free meal. It was a gamble. I didn't have to wait long before I heard a familiar keening cry overhead.

I opened one eye and saw those ripper claws
hurtling towards me.

I shouted as loudly as I could 'STOP!' as I jumped
up and ran round in circles, barking. The female kite
said,

'Mmmm, moving target!' but the male listened and
deflected her and they came to a quick halt on the
grass a few feet away from me.

'Phew, thank you both – that was close! I need
you to use the kite communication system to get a
message to Jory and Milva in Wiltshire, please. Tell
them Roro needs them and they must come at once!'

The kites took to the air without a backward glance.
I could sense the female was disappointed not to
be tucking into a tasty snack. No time to waste. The
kite's code of honour would hold them to delivering
the message probably via various pairs of kites over
other hunting grounds en route.

It was drizzling and I decided to go back underground to wait. I hid in the first secret chamber so I could keep an eye on the captive dragons. I'd like to have gone and retrieved the packet of biscuits from the ledge but decided against it. The candle spluttered and fizzled out. Darkness engulfed the chamber. I thought happy thoughts.

I heard heavily booted footfall approach from within the chamber and I kept very still and quiet although my heart was thumping loudly in my chest. There must be another entrance perhaps through the castle ruin itself.

The collector had returned and played his torch beam around the walls of the chamber. I hardly dared breathe. The dragons grew agitated and I could hear them flapping and straining on their leashes. The man threw them something – presumably food – and the phoenix started up her pitiful noise from the top of the tower again.

'Don't know what a phoenix eats,' muttered the

collector and he crumbled up some biscuits from the packet and threw them into the base of the tower, out of reach of the dragons.

'Not for you, for the bird,' he admonished gruffly.

Then he went out again.

I went back out through the fox covet to watch where he went and to wait for Jory and Milva. Luckily they didn't take long – there must have been strong head winds assisting the bird flight.

'My, my, Roro, you have been quite a little detective since you helped free the unicorns,' said Milva.

'What do you need us to do?' said Jory.

'I think there's a captive phoenix in there,' I said, pointing to the tower, 'and two tethered dragons – mind though, they're a bit snappy. Can you free them all whilst I think of a way of detaining the man who captured them? There's access through this fox hole but there must also be another way in from the ruined castle.'

'We will find it, don't you worry.'

The kites flew off accepting instructions without question and set to work. I'd told them to use their talons and sharp beaks to free the dragons and the unhappy phoenix.

Now I must carry out my newly hatched plan.

I trotted down the road and let some unsuspecting sheep out from a farmer's field by opening the gate. A passing motorist called the police – it was lucky he had mobile signal – and they quickly sent a couple of officers to round them up.

My plan was working.

Wandering sheep could be a bit of a nuisance roaming about the country lanes, but there was no traffic about, only the one Sunday driver who had

The Secret Adventures of Rolo

alerted the police – I had already carried out a hasty risk assessment before I released them as I wouldn't have wanted to cause an accident or harmed the sheep in any way.

Naturally I appeared on the scene and helped the police with the rounding up as I am originally from Wales and fancy myself as a bit of a sheepdog.

When the sheep were safely but rather indignantly penned – they knew after all that I was responsible for letting them out in the first place – I barked repeatedly at the policemen and eventually got them to follow me up the hill to the ruins of the castle. The collector was just getting out of his jeep as we arrived and PC Jones and PC Davies assumed they had found the culprit who had let the sheep out.

They arrested the collector there and then, believing they had caught him red handed in the act of stealing the sheep. The trailer he had used to move the unicorns was discovered in the bushes with a bit of help from yours truly and the police were convinced this was evidence enough to take the strange man in for questioning.

The collector didn't see me at first and I was wondering whether Jory and Milva had managed to free the dragons.

Suddenly I saw the magnificent sight of a pair of dragons, one red and one white, burst out from the ruined castle and swoop off into the trees. Luckily the policemen were too busy arguing with the collector – who was of course denying all charges of sheep rustling – to see the dragons overhead. The arresting officer had the collector's arm bent tightly around his back so he couldn't struggle. He used his free arm to feel in the man's coat pocket for possible concealed weapons. He pulled out my jewel collar.

'Well, well, what have we here then?'

I barked frantically again and the smart policeman said,

'Is this yours little dog? Is that why you led us to catch this sheep stealer? Did the nasty man take your collar?'

The collector snarled at me and I couldn't say whether he recognised me or not. I suspect we Jack Russells all look the same to humans.

I started dancing round and round in a circle, barking with excitement at seeing the jewel collar again as I thought it was lost forever and my adventuring days were over. In truth I was also trying to distract the policemen as I could see that the phoenix had been released from the tower and Jory and Milva were chasing her off up into the clouds, her twirling tail feathers trailing behind her. Phew, I think our little secret went undiscovered.

The policeman restraining the collector handed the collar to his colleague and the young PC knelt down on the ground. There was nothing else I could do but meekly go to him and have it fastened around my neck. He slid the jewel round to the base of my throat. Uh oh – I knew of course what would happen next!

I felt a familiar tingling all over my furry little body and had to get away from the scene as fast as my short legs would carry me because I knew I was turning into a dragon and there was nothing I could do to stop it!

'There you go, take yourself off home then, good job, thanks for your help little fella,' called the policeman after me as he re-joined his colleague who was pushing the criminal's head down to get him safely inside the back of the police car.

'P.C. Jones do you think that little dog's alright? He looks a bit strange to me and he's taken off in rather a hurry.'

'Don't you worry about the dog P.C Davies, he is a feisty little terrier and that breed can take care of themselves. Let's get this shifty one down to the station.'

In my half-dog, half-dragon state I managed to hide among the ruined walls from where I listened to the retreating nee-naw, nee-naw of the police car siren as it returned to the station with the collector safely stowed on board.

Delighted as I was to be reunited with the jewel collar I really needed to get it off as quickly as possible! My unwanted transformation was complete and I was Rodor the dragon once more.

I spied Reod and Alba circling behind the trees no doubt eyeing up the poor confused sheep and I flagged them down using the same tactics I had used to entice the kites.

275

The Secret Adventures of Rolo

Luckily there were still no visitors or dog walkers in the grounds on this dreary afternoon as they wouldn't have believed the sight of three dragons, a red one, a white one and a white, toffee and chocolate coloured one having a meeting among the castle ruins.

'Well, what have we here?' said Reod.

'Funny looking dragon if you ask me; not one of us!' chipped in Alba, sniffing me suspiciously.

'He's very small!' agreed Reod, 'bite-size in fact.'

'Listen you two, it's me, Rolo. The dog, you know, the one you've seen in countless adventures!'

'You don't look much like a dog to me!' sneered Alba, 'You've a crispier skin, I reckon.'

I quickly explained about the jewel collar, and how the gift from Father Christmas enabled me to have adventures in myths and legends and that I turned into a dragon when I wore it.

I asked them if they could please do me a really big favour and take the collar off so I could turn back into a dog.

They looked at each other and exchanged a few questioning glances and muttered doubtfully.

I heard Alba say,

'Well, if it's a trick we can easily overpower him.'

Reod smacked his lips menacingly and both dragons advanced on me, united for once; I kept my nerve as they approached. Using their dragon foreclaws surprisingly daintily, like pincers, they managed to unbuckle the collar and then stood back to watch what happened next.

My body started tingling and the scales became fur again and my tail shrank down to its usual waggy flag. The dragons stared in disbelief, possibly disappointed.

I thanked them politely and asked Reod if I could please have my collar back and when he held it out I took it from him with my teeth, barked my thanks again and ran back down the hill following the footpath and crossed the road carefully, heading straight back under the fence to the cheerful cook's house. Luckily there was no one around and I remembered the route. I was worried about the length of time I'd been away in case I had been missed.

By the time I reached the backdoor I could see the ladies were still in the same place I had left them – lounging on the sofas and by the looks of the debris on the low table they had drunk plenty of tea and scoffed a fair few cakes.

'Golly, Rolo, you've been out in the garden a long time. I'd completely forgotten about you! I suppose you would have barked sooner if you'd wanted to come in,' the smiley lady wrapped me in a towel and proceeded to wipe my feet and then give me a good brushing.

After all that fresh air you won't need much of a walk this evening, will you? Would you like your dinner?'

Before barking to be let in at the backdoor, I'd secreted the jewel collar behind a flower pot. I would have to remember to collect it later and hide it in my traveling cage which doubles as my bed when we go visiting.

At least the jewel collar was back in my possession. I would be sure to keep it safe until my next adventure.

Right now I was ready to eat and then snuggle up with the smiley lady and doze on her lap whilst she wittered away to her friend about things in her life that she considers exciting.

A few days later I overheard the smiley lady on the phone to the cheery cook, relaying what she'd heard from the floppy haired boy over dinner.

'Now apparently, after apprehending a suspected sheep rustler, two policemen stumbled upon a series of underground chambers beneath the ruins of Montgomery Castle, possibly dating back to the time of religious persecution. Can you believe it? And we were there! Did you find them when you went down that fox hole, Rolo?'

Oh, smiley lady, you really have no idea.

Postscript

I see the River Kennet sparkling silver below as it meanders through the valley. The river is home to many carefree trout being watched over by hungry kingfishers and herons. The waterway is guiding me home.

Looking down, I can just about make out paw prints on the muddy footpath, and there is Chickpea shut in her back garden running round and round in a circle barking up at me.

Onwards I go, over the tops of the winter-bare trees, soaring over fallow fields and the little church where the smiley lady goes, and on across the school playground. One pupil spots me, tells his friend and word goes around like wildfire – the entire playground is a sea of waving and smiling primary school children, calling my name and pointing up to the sky. I wonder if they can really see me or are they imagining that they can?

I fly over the College grounds where Marlborough

Castle once proudly stood. Someone is painting white lines to mark out the boundaries of the rugby pitch, ready for the new term and fiercely fought inter-school matches.

Now, along the main road and round the square tower of St Peter's church, location of the Chilvester Passage and where I interrupted Thomas Wolsey's ordination and caught some robbers.

Around the subtle curve of the High Street, over the rooftops of the shops and houses, and below me I can see the canopies of the market stalls. I remember that this was where The Great Fire of Marlborough nearly wiped out the town and the consequent ban on thatched roofs, past St Mary's where I rescued the cat family, across the Common where I showed the medieval greyhound how to find rabbits to feed the hungry people, and at last to the forest to find Athelstan, tree dragon and guardian of the time tunnel.

I can just about make out the woodland folk from

up here as I start my descent. Da is looking up to the sky in the wrong direction and Yulia is holding her lantern and waving her free arm as if she is an air traffic controller guiding me safely down.

And there in the forest is the floppy haired boy. He is aware of something descending from the sky and screws up his eyes to focus. He sees a small tri-coloured dragon coming in to land. When the jewel collar is removed, the dragon turns into his beloved dog. The floppy haired boy can hardly believe his eyes!

I am tucked under a blanket in my basket fast asleep and dreaming. I love having dragon adventures, but I also enjoy being an ordinary little Jack Russell. Of course my owners have no idea what I am secretly up to at night when they are fast asleep.

I wonder what Athelstan has in store for me next?

'Jewel Dog and the Dragons'

The Secret Adventures of Rolo

Characters

<u>The dogs</u>

Rolo – rescue Jack Russell and time traveller. Hero of the book. Also variously known as Little Pup, Paddy Paws, docga, Lucky/hund, kyon and, as well as Rodor, drakon and Derkomai (Ancient Greek)

Chickpea – female Jack Russell. Rolo's friend.

Merlin, Juno, Maisie, Suzy, Sparkle and Tia – Rolo's friends and neighbours

Beauty – black Labrador (blog #1)

Rayaan and Noor – Sheikh Zayed's salukis (Chapter 5)

<u>The humans</u>

Smiley lady – Rolo's owner

Floppy haired boy – smiley lady's son

Grandad Polo – smiley lady's father

Cheerful cook – smiley lady's friend (Chapter 6)

Northern twin – another friend of the smiley lady (blog #9)

<u>The woodland folk</u>

Yulia – a tiny girl who lives in the forest and lights

Rolo's way on his time traveling adventures

Da – Yulia's great great great great grandfather and great source of nature and sayings

Bubo – the owl

The dragons

Athelstan – tree dragon and guardian of the time tunnel in the forest

Rhydian – Welsh dragon, calls Rolo 'Ci Em' which means Jewel Dog

Gwyn – baby dragon hatched in an airing cupboard by Rolo (Book 3)

Alba – English white dragon

Reod – Welsh red dragon

Rodor – Rolo's dragon name (Anglo Saxon meaning 'of the sky')

Other Characters

Jory and Milva – red kites (Chapter 1)

Tommy and Jimmy – soldiers in the trenches (Chapter 3)

King Alfred the Great – Saxon king

Hilde – a kitchen servant in King Alfred's household (Chapter 4)

Sheikh Zayed bin Sultan al Nahyan – first president
of the United Arab Emirates (Chapter 5)
King Odysseus, Helen of Troy, Charon, Cerberus,
Hades and Persephone – characters from Greek
mythology (Chapters 8 & 10)
Aesop – legendary Greek storyteller (Chapter 11)
The collector – characterised by his battered top hat
and long dark coat (Chapter 13)

Other mythical creatures (Chapter 13)
Sigil, Estar, Sable, Roshan, Silvesse, Arryn, Helios,
Erwyn, Elmas, Jaden, Jonty and Rune – unicorns
Phoenix

Previous adventures mentioned
Peter Long – medieval villager (Book 1)
Brutus – Roman dog in Pompeii (Book 2)
Flint – Amesbury Archer's dog in the Bronze Age
(Book 2)
Guy Fawkes (Book 3)
Thomas Wolsey's ordination (Book 1)
The Great Fire of Marlborough (Book 1)